Love Dreams
A NOVEL

Sherry Lucille

Inspiring Destiny Press
MADISON, WISCONSIN

First Edition

ISBN-13: 978-0615741444

ISBN-10: 0615741444

This novel is a work of fiction. Names, characters, places, and
incidents are either the product of the author's imagination or
are used fictitiously. All characters are fictitious, and any
similarity to people living or dead is purely coincidental.

Published by:

Inspiring Destiny Press

www.sherrylucille.com

Cover art by Hannah Sandvold
hsgraphics.blogspot.com
hcsandvold@gmail.com

DEDICATION
To Jehovah Jireh

Mothers

Mabel Gaines

Viola Edmonds, Ada Lucille, Verline Gee Fleming,
Lola Jones, Ardenia Malone, Jackie Gee, Edna Raja
&
Mother Gaddis

CAST OF CHARACTERS

James "Jimmy" Johnson
Jilted lover of Shelly

Kimberlane Steel
Pennsylvania socialite

Mike Swane
James' longtime friend

Joseph
Steel Manor servant

Eleanor Steel
Kimberlane's Pennsylvania aunt

Edward Steel
Kimberlane's grandfather

Mama Rose
Everybody's grandmother

Mark Schultz
Bane of James' existence

$P_{ROLOGUE}$

❧

Pennsylvania 1957~Kimberlane
What Is This Place?

"MISS SMITH."

Nobody called her that, and tonight it made her stomach crawl and sent shivers up her spine. She pretended to sleep, not seeing city turn to country, brick buildings to trees. The stranger who met her at the train station was now extending his long fingers asking her to take his hand. Despite the silky comfort of the beige seats, the smooth ride of the luxury car and the husky assurance of his deep voice, fear surrounded her.

"Er, Mr. Joseph, I'm only fifteen." Her plaid skirt stuck to her thighs as she scooted away from him and further into the protection of the car.

"Ma'am?"

"I mean, I'm too young to work here by myself." Her tongue was dry and her hungry belly churned. Off in the distance, the sun was dipping in an angry sky. It made the sight before her look even more strange. A huge monster of a building stood high and wide. It didn't make any sense, none at all.

"If my uncle E and aunt Mattie owe some money—"

"Ma'am," the gray-haired man was impatient now, "your family…"

Family. Kimberlane could no longer hear him; just days ago the only family she knew consisted of her aunt Mattie and uncle E. Who here could she possibly be related to? Was her dead mother alive after all? An odd urge to laugh warred with the sick feeling in her stomach.

His long arm was in the car now. There was no escape. She squeezed her eyes tight and allowed herself to be pulled from the car.

Chicago 1957~James
Just Practice

Captains of Industry, Captains of War, Captains of High School Football Teams. Jimmy hadn't thought of it much but why shouldn't he? If anyone deserved to be… *Better not get ahead of yourself*, Jimmy thought. He was a practical kid and didn't much care for daydreams. The August sun was driving sweat into his face as he lumbered onto Franklin High's football field. Freshmen were jetting back and forth, anxious to prove themselves. He was a veteran and a good one—no need to show off.

"Hey, Jimmy!" Mike barreled onto Franklin field, pushing Tim into the sidelines and shoving a tired and sweaty Greg. Excitement gathered as he ran.

"Did you hear the news?!" He pumped his mammoth fist.

"What news, big guy?" Jimmy snapped his towel at Mike's head. "Slow down before you break somebody." Jimmy—James Johnson—and Mike had become an unlikely duo. Jimmy was tall and quiet and Mike was big and roared like a lion. Franklin High was integrated, but barely. James and Mike tried to work around it.

"What news?"

"The coaches are considering you for a team captain."

"Yeah, and Arkansas will one day have colored and white kids sitting side by side singing 'Kumbaya'. I wouldn't bet on it, Mike."

"Jimmy, this is Chicago, not Arkansas. Your family came back here for a change. And things are changing. Besides, everybody knows what you can do."

"And Mark, Tony, George, David? What about them?"

"They're good," Mike admitted.

"Yeah, and some are better than good and they're—"

"Don't say it, Jimmy."

"White! They're white and even if I play better, get along with people better, even if I'm smarter on and off the field…"

"I know, I know. But the guys all voted…"

Jimmy shook his head and kicked a stray uniform bag out of their way.

"Give it time to play out, Jimmy. I think you're wrong this time." Mike laid his big hand on Jimmy's shoulder. Jimmy smiled despite himself.

"Okay, big guy, let's wait and see how it plays out."

Chicago 1957~Mike
Nightmares

Sleep…who could sleep? Dragging their feet…why? Where'd she go? Drifting, slowly drifting. Reluctantly Mike's eyes fluttered and sealed. Quick twist right. Faster, left. He bolted up. He was dreaming again, an ugly harassing dream.

"Get her!" yelled David, running as fast as he could down their South Side sidewalk. The burning heat seared them and bounced off her yellow dress. Their small prey pretended to be brave as they closed in. Her fluffy head snapped over one shoulder then the other. She was scared, walking fast. Her thin brown legs picking up speed as the distance between her and them became short. Outnumbered and outsized, she squeezed between two buildings and ran full out. Mike's stomach churned at the thought of how fragile and helpless she was. He was sorry, so sorry.

It was his concern for his best friend, Jimmy Johnson, which caused him to have this dream again. She had never told Jimmy about him. She was a good girl, a very good girl.

Pennsylvania 1957~Kimberlane Home

Joseph led the way up the wide chalk-colored steps. If it took him two strides, it took Kimberlane three to conquer each one.

"You're shaking, miss. Can I help you?" The older man looked down at her.

"I—I'm fine," she repeated.

But she wasn't. She tried thinking about her home in Chicago. She was standing in her kitchen watching her aunt boil potatoes.

"Mattie," she moaned in the back of her throat. At first she thought the whole thing was a joke.

Then Mattie said, "They want you now," crumbling a letter in her hand and folding Kimberlane into her arms.

"What? Who wants me?"

Mattie, who was a woman of few words, pushed Kimberlane back and stared at her with those big cow's eyes.

"Who wants me?" Kimberlane questioned again.

"Them. The other side of your family," she snapped.

What other side, Kimberlane wanted to know. Mattie was her mother's older sister. She had never even heard of her dad, though she knew everybody had one. She made the mistake of asking about him once. Mattie and E pounced on her like she'd lit the house on fire.

"There's nothing I can do about it," her aunt mumbled, walking away. "Better pack your stuff."

You're sending me to the unspeakable? she had

thought. Why didn't Mattie tell her more? Uncle E just sat there, his wheelchair rolled tight against the window seal, his shoulders hunched, his slick head looking away—out, out into the darkness.

"We owe them," he groaned. "Better do as your aunt says."

Days had passed but she could still see them both scared and not in control. Mattie had always been in control. Who were these people that they could frighten her aunt? The memory pinched her chest.

Finally, she and Joseph were at the top of the stairs and at the gigantic red door. It opened slowly. Joseph ushered her into a room that went on and on. *How could people own a house this big and not be able to put anything in it?* she thought. Since there was nothing to see on the floor, her eyes traveled up and up and up. A chandelier-thing full of glittering glass ornaments hung from the ceiling. If there had been a ladder high enough to reach it, she figured she and four or five friends could spin from it without bumping into a thing. Kimberlane, known for being big and brave, suddenly felt small and alone. This was no fairy wonderland.

"Come along, miss." Joseph's commanding voice brought her back to the elegant museum and the coming meeting with 'the other side'. Again, he extended his large hand. "Miss? Miss, you're walking backwards."

Her eyes dropped to see her feet retracing their steps, backing over the smooth black and ivory pearled marble beneath her.

"Please, ma'am, your coat." Joseph creased her shoulder. "There is really no need to be afraid." His voice was calm and steady. Her breathing slowed a little as a thin, kind-looking man approached her.

"Hi, I'm Kimberlane. Are you my—" Joseph's glare cut into her speech.

"Joseph, is that you? Have you got her?" A beautiful angel voice sang from around one of the floor-to-ceiling light-gray pillars.

"Yes, ma'am." Joseph echoed into the giant gold room surrounding them.

Kimberlane craned her neck to see a lovely fox-haired woman prancing in her direction. Her thin pink and cream hands were primming and fussing with the belt on her satiny blue dress, which made a bell above her long slender legs.

Two steps behind her came a man torn right out of the Sears catalog. He moved quickly despite his sugar-cane walking stick and the gray at the sides of his sandy temples. He pressed past the pointy-faced willow woman and pushed his hand at her.

"Hello, Kimberlane—I am your grandfather."

The room spun, her heart stopped, and everything went black.

Chicago 1957~James
Team

"I've been polling the team," Mike yelled, loping out of the locker room doors into the warm air.

"Me, too," Jimmy joined. "You gonna make it, man?" He stopped so his friend could catch up with him.

"Sure. Slept like crap though." They walked

together.

"Me, too. But I asked a couple of guys…"

"Yeah?" Mike brightened. "And they said?"

"They said they're votin' for me."

"You starting to believe?" Together they ran onto the sun-soaked field.

"A little." Jimmy pinched his fingers together, squinting through the slit. "A little."

Pennsylvania 1957~Kimberlane Pain

"No!" Kimberlane heard herself shriek. "You can't shoot!"

William Tell threw his arm back over his shoulder, reached into his goatskin sack and re-loaded. Whoosh—the arrow missed the apple altogether and hit right between her eyes.

"It hurts," she moaned, expecting no one to hear through the thick shroud that surrounded her. The stabbing pain in the middle of her face caused her lids to quiver. A thin web covered her eyes. She could just make out fuzzy stone statues standing guard over her as she lay floating.

"Who's there?" she groaned.

"It's me, dear. Eleanor." A cloudy version of the pretty woman leaned in. "You remember the lady in blue. It really is my best color—"

"Eleanor," a strained voice complained.

Someone was touching her hand now, stroking it. "Phillip, come here. Your patient is coming around."

"You shouldn't have done it, Eleanor. It wasn't

right." The croaking thin voice was speaking in the distance.

"Quiet, Phillip. She's sedated, not dead. And didn't I just say she's coming around?"

"Where am I?" Kimberlane spoke, not sure her muttering was breaking through the pain and the thin cool cloth laid over the middle of her face.

"You're here in our home, your home." Kimberlane felt her nails dig into the cushiony covers.

"I am your aunt Eleanor and this is our family physician, Dr. Phillip Lovejoy. It's all very shocking, isn't it? Didn't you know anything about us?"

"Here, let me get that," the man's voice echoed. The cloth was pulling away from her head.

Her eyes felt sticky and thick. She stretched and willed them to open wide. Throne-like chairs emerged and she could make out netting around her bed, and even in her haze she became incensed. This witch had to know she'd never so much as heard a peep about an Aunt Eleanor or 'that man' they were calling her 'grandfather' in her entire life, still didn't know what was really going on. One thing was for sure: her world had been turned upside down.

"What, what happened?" Her tongue was beefy, lazy, dry. It was hard to speak.

Eleanor laughed, "I'm sure you could be referring to any part of this situation, but let me start with the immediate. There will be plenty of time later for explaining the rest. You fainted as soon as you saw your grandfather." She laughed again. "He does have an imposing manner."

Young Kimberlane knew she was at the mercy of these fiends, but must she lay here and be insulted on top of everything else? This woman had to know that it was not her grandfather's imposing manner that had upset her.

"During your faint…uhumm," she cleared her throat. "On your way to the floor, you hit your face. I'm afraid surgery was—"

"Eleanor, this is shameful!"

What? What was shameful?

"Let me handle this, Phillip," Eleanor grunted.

"You see, my dear, your face was not only injured in the fall, but disfigured. I'm afraid reconstructive surgery was required. Our dear friend here…" The words Kimberlane heard were murky and garbled. But Eleanor continued, "…was happily just coming for his weekly visit when you arrived; very fortuitous. I'm sure you will agree when you are well enough to see his handiwork."

Kimberlane's head felt like it was being forced into one of those tools used to squeeze wood into place while it was hammered, hacked and nailed. Suddenly, gushing water leapt to her eyes. It wasn't bad enough that she was in this strange place with relatives she didn't know or recognize. Now she had been injured and fixed. Would she even recognize herself?

Chicago 1957~Mark Regret

Mark sat alone in the darkened locker room, running his hand through his hair, trying to figure out what he was feeling. He had asked his crew who they would vote for, for captain and they all said him, then Jimmy

Johnson. He liked the boy, he really did, and no one deserved to be captain as much as he did. He was surprised, that's all. There had never been a Negro captain of the Franklin Falcons. And Mark had to admit it; if it were any Negro but Jimmy, he'd actually be glad. But this guy riled him in every way.

And he seemed to have the one thing Mark never could. Not that he wanted her, mind you. She was a skinny little thing with an awkwardly shaped bottom…when had that happened? He remembered how they played and even wrestled as children. She was his best friend then. He smiled. Now she was his nemesis. He scowled. Always challenging him to do better, be better. He punched the locker. Who the hell did she think she was? Oh yeah, the most uppity little colored girl in all of Franklin High. He didn't care what she did or who she liked. So why, why, did it make him queasy to see her with Jimmy? And now he was going to be captain, too? Well, it just didn't seem fair, that's all. He stripped off his cleats and dirty socks.

Why were the coaches taking so long to decide something that should have been done the first week of practice? The whole team had voted and it was no secret that their favorites were him, David and Jimmy. Andrew was the coach's nephew. Why was he asked to stand? He was a milquetoast: pale, damp and limp. Just plain boring. According to Mike's unofficial poll, nobody had even mentioned him.

Jimmy would be the first of them, then. Others had deserved it, but nobody was willing to go out on a limb for them. Jimmy…he was different. He'd be the first Negro player to be captain. He was good. Mark shook his head. Okay, better than good. If he'd just leave Shelly alone…

Mark threw his gym bag against the lockers and stormed from the locker room.

"Jimmy! Jimmy! David! Mark!" The chants flew as the boys assumed to have received the most team votes marched up to the front of the gym along with George and Andrew.

"Hold your cheers, guys," Coach Martin said. "We had a hard, hard decision to make. Never in Franklin history have we had so many talented kids on this team. As you know, it's our tradition to choose four team captains. The young men standing here today represent our best: strong, dedicated, athletic and academic."

"Jimmy, Jimmy! Mark, Mark!" The continued yells drowned out the coach's speech. He raised his hands to silence them. "We hear you. We hear you!" There was laughter in his voice. The boys before him smiled—all five. Three knew why they were there. George Olephant looked down at his shoes and shuffled. Andrew eyed the ceiling and wrung his jersey as if he'd stolen something.

"This year we are trying something new…"

A deadly hush fell over the gym.

"NO!!!"

The collective crescendo was deafening. Coach Martin took a step back, his face twisted into a blotchy knot of worry and amazement.

"Hold on, boys," he peered over his shoulder at the other coaches who looked the other direction. "Let me explain…"

Mark could barely believe what he was hearing. His dream was coming true. Jimmy would not be captain—only he and David would. All three of the other boys—Jimmy, George, and Andrew—would be assistants. All new positions, created because of the large number of 'talented' kids. "This is crap," he heard himself say aloud.

Everyone was mad, even David who seemed to have no use for coloreds.

"Jimmy, wait up, man," Mark said as the coach quickly dismissed the angry and confused boys. Some huddled, talking loudly. The colored boys ran to Jimmy but were waved off by Mike and Fred standing guard.

"Whad'ya want, Mark?" Jimmy yelled over his faithful watchmen.

"Mark, get back. This is not the time," Mike defended.

"Want to rub it in? Come on, let's do it." Jimmy threw down his bag.

"Hey, wait a minute. I'm on your—"

"—my side." Jimmy stepped toward Mark, pushing Mike and Fred away. "Yeah, right. It was no secret you didn't want me…" Jimmy glared at Mark, then turned. "Never mind."

"Hold on, Jimmy, this isn't…" Mark saw Mike try to touch Jimmy, getting his hand shoved away twice before Jimmy stalked off alone.

This was nasty. It stung like the comments his father had once made about his friendship with

Shelly. *There must be something that can be done*, Mark thought. *There must be something.*

"Can I talk to you, Jimmy?"

Jimmy wanted to ignore the veiled plea but turned sharply into the office just off the gym as he made his way out the door.

"No, coach, it's not necessary," he paused briefly to say.

"We did everything we could, son."

"That's…B.S." Jimmy moved toward the desk, still talking in a low rumble.

"Wud you say?" Coach Martin pushed back in his chair, staring wearily up at the boy towering above him.

Jimmy James Johnson did not relent. " I said," he doled out slowly, "that's bullshit and you know it. I'm the best." He pounded his fist on the desk between them. "Everybody knows it. You know it. Even I know it," Jimmy hissed.

"Okay, no more 'bullshit' as you put it." Coach Martin carefully placed his hands on the desk and pushed to his feet. "We couldn't do it. The kids may be ready, but the adults are not."

James stiffened, turned his back, and walked toward the office door.

"We still need you."

"I know," Jimmy said, not bothering to turn around.

"What are you gonna do?"

"I DON'T KNOW," he spat, yanking the door, shaking its frame.

Pennsylvania 1957~Kimberlane
New

In and out of twilight sleep: partly because she was tired, partly because she was perplexed. Twisting and turning in covers too pretty to sleep on, too comfortable not to. Bandages removed and replaced. Up and washed. Body squeezed into new expensive outfits: sunset yellow, crisp orange. The crushing pain above her lip: all but gone. Days collapsed into weeks, weeks into months; and finally the butterfly of many colors emerges from its cocoon.

"Parlez-vous francais?" the nosey Mrs. Marvel asks.

"Oui oui, Madame Marvel," Kimberlane answers, sitting on a beautifully tufted blue rosewood settee, sipping English tea with her pinky extended toward the vaulted ceiling.

"I moved to Provence from Sicily with my mother's family when I was a few years old."

The 'move' to France was necessitated by Kimberlane's inability to learn Italian quickly.

"Why haven't we ever heard of you before now?"

Because my aunt Eleanor made this story up when I was kidnapped from Chicago nine months ago.

"What's that, dear? I'm sorry, I didn't get that."

Eleanor swooped in, "My father, you know how he can be. He was so disturbed by his only son marrying without his permission. Then there was the pain of losing my brother and his young wife so abruptly. He just couldn't bring himself to talk about them."

"Yes," Kimberlane jumped in, "I never knew my parents."

"Never?" Mrs. Marvel's eyes bugged, nearly popping their sockets.

"Hardly. She hardly knew her parents," Eleanor spat, choking on her tea. "Careful, Kimberlane, you wouldn't want Mrs. Marvel here to get the wrong impression."

"No," Kimberlane's hand flew to her chest, "we wouldn't want that." She stood, abandoning her petits fours and china cup. The lies came so easy for Eleanor and they were beginning to come easier for her, too. Every day, in that part of the house where discreet guests were kept, they practiced: she, her grandfather, and her aunt. They synchronized their stories, sometimes laughing at the absurdity of it all. Her grandfather seemed equally amused at her ability to pick up French and Eleanor's ability to spin plausible lies.

With a new face emerging, a steady diet of watercress and cucumber sandwiches, being told over and over again who she now was while having her every need met, Kimberlane began to feel and look like a 'Steel'. But peering just beneath her weary brown eyes was the Kimberlane of old, and though she wanted to believe that this was a dream come true, something deep inside echoed…just the beginning of sorrows, just the beginning.

1

❦

Chicago 1969

KIMBERLANE LEFT HER HOTEL early and walked on the hard gray pavement until her black pumps needle-pricked her toes. The leafless April trees offered little cover from the whirling winds that made her eyes tear as she looked up to find herself on familiar Chicago streets. Everything was mossy-gray or brown. The dingy snow was dotted with specks of dust and dirt, a visible representation of how she felt inside.

Twelve years ago when her aunt told her to pack her things and she'd be moving to Pennsylvania, she thought Mattie had finally developed a sense of humor.

"Sure," she had responded, glancing quickly from sweeping the stringy-yarned carpet of the living room to the yellow kitchen. "Who's going to clean up for you when I'm gone?" Her smile was big but Mattie did not smile back.

"This is no joke," she had said, flinging a serving spoon into the sink. She pulled a fancy sheet of paper from her pocket. "They want you and they want you

17

now." Mattie had given her a quick hug. "The other side. Your father's people. Damn, I hate the well-to-do. Anyway," she turned her back, "they said they'll tell you what you need to know when you get there."

"When I get where? You really want me to leave?" Kimberlane remembered feeling empty and scared, her hands limp, dangling from the unanswered need to hold onto Mattie.

"I'm sorry, Kimberlane, it's what they want. I can't say no to them. I'll help you get your stuff together."

All the pain of being raised by her restrained aunt and mousey uncle came crashing in. Whatever they were or were not, they were familiar. But her new family needed her, so she was stripped and shipped to a place she had only heard about in geography class.

She was fifteen then, and now at the age of twenty-seven, she again asked herself, *Why, Lord? Why am I so unlovable?* Before she could retrieve the kerchief from her black patent bag, the day answered her with a warming smile. Small sea-colored buds peeked from behind a large tree to reveal the beginnings of new life. It was enough—the bliss of bright sun, the green of birth and a new breeze blowing. Life held promise she wouldn't give up. Not yet.

The clash of cymbals and the heavy bass of rhythmic drums wailed to her. Kimberlane turned toward the cacophony that summoned. There were two boys—one slight and yellow with fuzzy hair and the other tall, maybe seventeen, a common-looking boy—moving instruments from under a large painted sign hanging from an ornate silver chain which read "Mt. Prospect".

She remembered seeing the church years ago

though she doubted she had ever been in. Her aunt and uncle said religion was a personal thing. So personal apparently that they didn't talk about it even to each other.

That all changed when she moved away from Chicago. Her grandfather—a man who surrounded himself with Egyptian scrolls, transcripts of African oral traditions, and spiritual literature from around the globe—was something of a religious scholar, always citing some passage or another in theoretical terms. It was one of their stranger meetings when he called her into his room a week ago.

"Kimberlane, sit by me." He patted the rich red blanket that was tucked tightly by his arm. He was hunched up on his elbows and his regal silver hair was neatly combed back as if Miriam, his personal maid, had been in to dress it especially for her visit.

Rather than sit where he suggested, Kimberlane had pulled over one of his giant chairs with the gilded gold frame surrounding the deeply cushioned back and sat close enough to hear his quiet but impassioned speech.

"Kimberlane, how many years has it been now?" Her grandfather wound his mouth into a serious twist. She didn't know what he meant exactly: how many years had his daughter, her aunt Eleanor, been the bane of her existence? How many summers had she been sent to the rejuvenation spa, a.k.a. fat pig reduction joint? How many years had 'Dr. Killjoy', as she liked to call him, performed his wonders on her at the behest of Aunt Eleanor?

"Kimberlane, please do try and pay attention. I am asking you a very serious question with very serious implications," he cautioned, drawing her back into his query.

"About twelve years, Grandfather. That's how long I've lived here."

"That's better." He smiled at the realization that she was ready to play his game of unravel-the-mystery.

Everything was so formal in this house. Aunt Mattie had howled over her descriptions of ceilings tall enough for a slide and swing set to be erected in the living room. Kimberlane told her about being lost in the house and crying for someone to come and find her. When one of the neighbor girls had suggested a walk in the dense woods that adjoined their two homes, she had glared at her thinking, hadn't this girl ever heard of the boogieman? The first time Kimberlane had made a call home with these stories, Mattie said, "Girl, quit your lyin' before I come up there and beat the stew out of you." She was joking, Kimberlane knew, but with a kind of laughing sadness in her voice. She never hung up without saying, "I love you, and I'm praying for you." Words Kimberlane had rarely heard when she actually lived with her first aunt and uncle in Chicago. This all happened before her new aunt Eleanor discovered her calls home and decided that 'outside' influences were detrimental to her development as a Steel.

"And have you enjoyed your time with us?" Her grandfather's stare was piercing her.

The truth or a lie, the truth or a lie? "Yes, of course, I have, Grandfather. You are my family."

"Yes, exactly, and this has been your oasis." Kimberlane practically choked on that bit of absurdity. Instead, she averted her eyes and kept her silence.

"Now, dear, you will find water in a desert place. I want you to return...hooooooome." The word echoed long and hard, like an all-encompassing black hollow with a jagged boundless boulder at its end. She was hurling toward it as it rose up to meet her, hitting her right between the eyes.

Kimberlane uncrossed her legs and felt her back slump and head drop, as all the air rushed from her lungs. She was about to laugh her most hideous and profound laugh, the one she had reserved for being wrenched out of her original home and told to go someplace else. She looked at his face. His forehead was folded with three deep crevasses caused by the arching of his bushy brows; his mouth was turned down on one corner and his nostrils flared. He wasn't joking. Kimberlane now noticed the three incredibly large books on his bed. Her grandfather who had more money than anyone she knew, things he had no use for, and people ready to do his will great or small, now wanted to give her training in religion. The absurdity seemed never to end.

Kimberlane blinked several times and blew a growling breath. Seven days since her departure, yet nothing she did wiped away the all-too-fresh memory of that conversation with her grandfather. Still trying, she turned her attention back to the boys moving the musical instruments as they rolled them on carts. Specks of baby green grass struggled to shine beneath the melting snow while the boys struggled to get their cargo down the slick hill to the lower entrance. Was there going to be a concert later that day? Maybe she'd stroll back after a couple of hours and see. She didn't have anything else to do.

Kimberlane hadn't noticed that she had

inadvertently moved quite close to the commotion in her attempts at spying. When she turned to leave, she nearly trampled a young tree. In the old days that tree would have been laid to waste, she mused, self-depreciation peppering her thoughts. It was an odd little thing, sort of in the way. In addition to new sprouts, two dead-looking, shriveled purple berries hung, refusing to yield to the new life coming. Strange, she thought, remnants from a fall twig left over from seasons past and refusing to drop. Why didn't they just let the old life go and give way to the new? Kimberlane reached to pluck them from their precarious perch when she spied a lone man walking with his head down and his hands shoved deep into his dark pant pockets. He paced laboriously toward a side door of the church. She looked back at the berries and suddenly just couldn't pluck them.

2

❧

An April Wedding

JAMES WALKED UNDER the heavy medieval archway and into Mt. Prospect's side door. He had pushed his hands deep into his pockets so no one would see his clenched fists. He held his head up high as he always did no matter how he felt inside. Perfect, there were still empty seats in back near Wilma. She was a big pretty girl. Or she would have been if the gap between her front teeth hadn't been so wide. Little gaps, cute; gaps wide enough to run trucks through, not really.

"Why, James Johnson, no one expected to see you here today." Her loud voice drew several stares. *Of course I'm here, Wilma. No one's going to be feeling sorry for me. Poor James couldn't face the wedding. Besides, what would people think if I wasn't here?* He had hoped that coming in late would have saved him this.

"James, honey, look at you." Rhonda, a very sweet-looking mouthy girl, sat in front of him with her elbow draped over the back of her pew peering directly into his eyes. "Black on black on black. Where did you find that shirt?" She was running her thin silky fingers down his chest. "If I didn't know better I'd think you were going to a funeral," she

23

teased.

"You shush now," Wilma countered. "For Jimmy James—"

"For me," James interrupted, "it's just a wedding of a…" Several people in the pews in front of him stopped talking and eased back. "And this shirt isn't black—it's dark gray." He clasped Rhonda's hand gently, patted it, gripped her shoulders with both hands and twisted her back toward the pulpit, causing the other guests to turn forward as well. He repositioned the knot of his black tie and re-tucked his gray shirt. He looked toward the front. The huge oak clock jeered 3:00, the bewitching hour.

Miss Lola, a jolly blonde dressed in a brightly flowered frock and a flimsily brimmed hat, came bouncing toward the piano. James fully expected her to be wearing floppy red clown shoes to match this circus. She plucked a traditional 'ting tha-da ting' to start the show. Bodacious ribbons around carnations hung on the end of pews and bounced in response to her raucous melody.

A deep groan rose to James' throat. Being attacked in an alley would feel better; in fact, having sub-machine gun rounds whir near his head had felt better. At least then he knew who his enemy was. In a million years, he never suspected it would be her, that she would be giving herself to Mark Schultz. His mood clouded as his eyes darted from one side to the other, hoping no one could see the gaping hole in the center of his pride. 3:10, little Darla Mason and Alexi Nicole Cassandra—nobody bothered trying to remember her last name—sauntered down the aisle. A diversion, thank God. They read First Corinthians, the book of love.

Such a beautiful day for such a dastardly deed. How could a princess of promise suddenly shift her shape into a vixen of deceit? Only months ago he had looked upon Mt. Prospect as the bastion of his own hopes. He would stand at its now shimmering altar and offer his hand in love to Shelly, the woman of his dreams. James bowed his head and allowed himself one second to appear human. His Shelly, she was radiant in her satiny white. This should have been their night of love and mischief. He had waited over a decade. What a fool? Yes, his papa did raise one. No matter how he tried, there was no denying that now.

His only consolation was neither his mother nor father were alive to see his shame. Heck, even if this had been his own wedding, his brother Jasper would likely not have bothered to return for it. So he was safe. Safe from the ridicule of everyone—except everyone in this church today. The church that his family had helped establish. The church which had nurtured Mama Rose and welcomed in the heathen Schultzes.

How could this happen to a man like him? A man who had so carefully planned and worked out every detail of his life, crossing all of the t's and dotting all the i's. He laughed—maybe that was it; he should have crossed some i's and dotted some t's. He sat rigid in the burgundy pews and waited. Everyone who knew him would be looking to see how the jilted 'ex' was taking it, and he wasn't taking it too good. No, he'd just sit here in the back and wait for the folly to begin. That's all it could be. She couldn't have thought this little travesty through. When had she had the time?

James looked up to see a very pregnant woman

loping down the ruby row in a pale boxy dress, her swollen fingers gripping a large bouquet. His ears perked to pay special attention to the next song which he had taken special pleasure in renaming "Here Comes the Bit…"

"Hi, handsome, haven't seen you in years."

"What, huh?"

A tall, dark model wearing a form fitting, silver-trimmed peach suit wiggled in next to him. "My God, you turned out good." Her hand flew to her stylish glasses, adjusting them so she peered directly into his eyes while smiling devilishly. "The epitome of handsome, you are. Tall…dark…and luscious." She drawled out the last three words. "Guess Shelly preferred tall dark and white. We knew in high school—"

"Pam?!"

"And I thought you'd forgotten." She kissed his cheek, leaving the lingering aroma of forbidden orchids. "If I wasn't going back to Europe on the next plane, we'd have to get reacquainted." She patted his thigh.

He didn't see that coming. Pam was gorgeous. What made her sit next to me?

"I hoped I'd see you here. When I walked in the door, I simply followed my hunch and looked to see who all the women were circling. And there you were."

James smiled. The attention of a beautiful woman should cheer him up. Right?

3

❧

The Trouble With James

"SIT DOWN, BOY. What's your trouble?"

Holding his jacket on his arm, James stepped over baskets filled with pies, fruits, homemade crocheting and other sundry goods laid in offering to the Reverend Mother. He couldn't think of anything he wanted to do less than visit with Rose today, but he needed some answers. Since he couldn't get them from Shelly, her grandmother would have to do. He laid his coat across the back of a chair and collapsed into the garishly red sofa, inadvertently stroking the plush velvet beneath his thumb. She hadn't yet removed the plastic from the companion chairs, which, thankfully, muted by the tan flower pattern meandering through them. It was all new, a celebration of her return to the neighborhood.

"My trouble?" he grunted, turning his head in the general direction of Jake Schultz's next-door home. Jake was Shelly's new father-in-law. The whole scene made James sick. Mama Rose stared into his eyes as if she could read the weariness of her would-be grandson-in-law. He crossed his legs and tried to drown out thoughts of Shelly by filling his lungs with the sweet smell of fresh corn bread baking not ten feet from him.

Rose had moved back only a month ago, but the entire neighborhood was sizzling. Their Matriarch had returned. It was amazing, really. Who else could stir such passion after being gone a decade? *Passion, Shelly, betrayal.*

"If you can't figure out my trouble, Miss Rose, you've lost your powers of clairvoyance," James spat toward the wise gray-brown-eyed woman sitting across from him.

"My powers of what? Boy, don't be cursing me and don't be snarling at me either."

James cut his eyes to a respectable stare as Mama Rose cautioned, pointing her all-knowing finger at his nose.

"I ain't got no powers of clair…clair…whatever you said. All of my understandin' come from the Lord, although it's rumored that I know everything." Her lips curled into a gentle smile as her strong brown hand gave him a pat. "I only know the things God gives me to know. And that's 'Mama' to you, Mr. J J Smarts."

Her plastic-covered chair squeaked as she got up to get a simmering cup of weak tea and a pat-of-oleo slathered corn bread, his favorites. He watched the deep bronze and milky white of the tea twist and turn into a creamy tan. His nose twitched at the bread's sweet aroma.

"Mama Rose, why do you call me that?" he edged, angry that he had stuffed his mouth full of the bread without thinking. "You know I prefer 'James': not 'Jimmy', not 'Jimmy-James', not 'J J' and certainly not 'J J Smarts'." He swallowed hungrily, trying to clear his throat. "I've worked hard to be respectable. I'm professional, conscientious, church-going—"

"Church-going?" Mama interrupted her own swallow of tea and narrowed her eyes.

"May I continue?"

"Don't let me stop you." Her hands were now on her hips.

"Where was I? Oh yes…church-going…" He gave her time for a rebuttal. There was none. "I contribute to the community, both with finances and deeds. I'm mannerable and—"

"—modest," Mama Rose supplied with a smirk.

"Yes, modest." He wanted to strangle her. "And I'm a decent-looking man."

"Now that's an under—"

"What's that, Mama? Your voice went quiet."

"Yes, James, you're most of that. But you're so straight."

"I don't get you."

"You're stiff, boy. Like a board." She was up collecting dishes and taking them to the kitchen.

"Oh," he laughed his cynical chortle, "so that's why she chose Schultz. He's more, more flexible, more fun. I thought it was because he's white."

"What?"

"Yes, that's right. But there's just one thing I don't understand. I don't understand how she…" He swallowed hard. "I hate them, Mama Rose—"

"Who?"

"Whites. Honkies. Crackers."

"Listen, boy—"

"No, you listen." James stood to emphasize his point. "I hate them." He paced and pointed in the general direction of Jake Schultz's home. "We've carried them on our backs since the beginning of time. They're nothing without us. We built this country and what do we get for it? The women they couldn't get by raping and stealing, they now get by marrying. What's that?"

"James, you're hurt, and hurt people say rash and stupid things."

"Oh, I'm stupid now, am I?"

"Will you stop for a minute and listen to me?"

Suddenly James felt deflated and worn. He plopped down on Rose's covered chair. It, too, squealed its disapproval. A Rose tirade, just what he needed to complete an otherwise perfect day.

She didn't disappoint. Before his head fell back in glib surrender, she lit in. "Honey, colored, white, it don't matter—we is all God's children. We all depend on one another. That's the way it's supposed to be. This earth is our home and we're family, that's all. The human family, His creation. And here's something else. It's a hard saying but you've got to hear it: Shelly didn't choose Mark. Fate chose them. God's hands was on them children, and three or four families were depending on that union for their own healing."

"Besides Papa-Jake Schultz being converted to the human race, who else was 'healed' as you put it?"

"Oh, I can see you're skeptical and hurt—"

"Hurt, over losing Miss Perfect? I don't think—"

"Careful, son, that's my grandbaby you threatening to trash."

"I'm sorry, Mama." He jumped to his feet. Defeated or not, he had, had all he could stand of the one-woman-reconciliation-patrol. "I'll talk to you another day. Mike's waiting for me."

"Mike? Would that be a Mr. Mike Swane?"

"Touché, Mama, touché." Mike was his best friend and Mike was...utterly and undeniably white.

4

໑

Do I Know You?

THE ELEVATOR OPERATOR was a tall Oriental man with slick black hair and a spotless white jacket. His long fingers extended way past his sleeves and would have made him look odd except his manner was so gracious. "Good morning, ma'am. Going out early, are we? I think it's going to be lovely."

"Why, yes," Kimberlane squinted at his lapel, "Huan. Are you going to be able to get out of this…elegant box to enjoy the day?"

He operated the silver metal handle like he was piloting a ship, deftly closing and opening the ornate doors before takeoff.

"Yes, Miss Steel. I work only half the day. The rest I'll spend with my wife and new son."

She closed her eyes and thought about the velvety interior of the luxurious lift her grandfather had had installed in their Pennsylvanian home just outside of Philadelphia.

"That's good, Huan," she said without opening her eyes. She thought to ask how he knew her name, but at a place like the Southton, the help would be paid to know who was there.

Since coming to Chicago over a month ago, she had been living in this expensive hotel and it was becoming impractical. She didn't know how long she was supposed to stay or how long she wanted to; but she knew her allowance, though sufficient, would last a lot longer if she used some economy. *Time to survey the land,* she thought as she stepped onto the literal red carpet and whirled through the revolving door.

Vacating her chic accommodations, she waltzed out into the day. The shriek of wolf calls assailed her ears. Shielding her eyes, she blinked against the silver-dipped orange sherbet sky. Men perched high up on the building across the street were tipping their hard hats at her perky-red, neatly fitting short dress and yelling sassy 'borderline' comments. She wasn't offended. They were admiring the European cut of her dress and the body fit for it, something she didn't take as lightly as some women might.

She walked for several blocks, noticing the not-so-subtle changes as she did. Manicured brick houses gave way to several apartment buildings unevenly dispersed between them: elaborate Romanesque-styled residences next to basic ordinary flat-faced homes. Before she knew it, the last South Side neighborhood she had lived in lay before her. She would soon be within spitting distance of her old home. It's funny—no matter how big a city is, your old neighborhood always appears smaller to your adult eyes. So many places were missing; Mr. Miles' neighborhood grocery store and Mrs. Cate's second-hand novelty store, gone. Franklin High had been expanded but Emerson Elementary was closed. It had been twelve years since she left and nothing was the same. Scratch that—the two faces approaching her looked vaguely familiar. She wasn't in the mood for reunions even if the two men staring at her were 'on the handsome side'. She took a few more steps before toppling. Wicked heels. "Hot pink devils," she was about to yell, as catcher's mitt hands made a cushion between her and the scratchy hard concrete below.

"Do I know you?" the gentle giant hummed, cradling her.

"That's the oldest line in the book, Mike. Remind me to help you with future come-ons. Please excuse my friend, miss. It's early and his brain's still fuzzy." The black man's lips parted ever so softly, revealing a sweet-naughty smile, bodacious and timid, while the white guy's large hands, which steadied her, held on overly long.

She gave a grateful smile, lifted her foot, adjusting her shoe and moved quietly away.

"I'm not joshing, James. I really think I know her."

"Of course you do," James doled out slowly, the handsome look of his mouth brightening.

Not knowing what to say, Kimberlane walked on until the pinching on the back of her heel became too much. Searching her purse, she located the rose colored Kleenex she had put there specifically for this reason. A barrier between her foot and that shoe.

"She's a real looker, isn't she?" Mike buzzed in the distance, arms crossing his chest, feet firmly planted.

"Looks a little high-echelon if you ask me, but go for it, man. What have you got to lose?" James returned. Neither appeared to care that she might still be able to hear them.

"What about you? Wouldn't you like to go for

it?" Since they had stopped with their backs to her but were still talking loudly enough for her to hear, she stopped to listen. After all, she was the topic.

"Mike, have you lost your mind? Have you ever known me to 'go for it' with a white woman? And besides, unlike some people, I try to do things decently and in order. Have you forgotten that it was only months ago that I was engaged?"

"James, be it far from me to point out the obvious, but you're only engaged if the lady in question is also engaged. Man, you have got to snap out of it. Shelly liked you, maybe even loved you. But unfortunately she loved him better."

"Love, huh? Well, I hope she gets what she bargained for."

"James, what's with this bitterness, man? I've never known you to wish anybody ill. You need to get a grip. There are plenty of 'quality women', as you like to put it. You've just got to put yourself out there and quit thinking there is this one perfect type. Open your eyes, James. Try to see what God has for you. Do it now, man. Don't miss a blessing right in front of you."

Kimberlane had heard enough. She walked away. Mike didn't know her. Even if he had known her years ago, he wouldn't know her now. Anyway, she was tired of being judged by how she looked. Bone tired.

It was when she first left Chicago in 1957 that she realized how she looked would be a problem for more than one reason. She had been in a deep sleep when the chugging and clanging of her Philadelphia-bound train made a sudden jerk. Her neck snapped forward and her eyes popped open. An old gray man sat across from her. His left eyebrow was arched and his heavily mustached upper lip pretended to conceal a smirky-toothed smile. His eyes danced with laughter. The conductor was teetering and bumping down the aisle; a pale blond woman wearing an old pea coat with badly patched sleeves stepped on the back of his heels as she followed.

"Right here, ma'am." he pointed to an empty seat next to a black woman wearing an A-line beige suit and expensive-looking shoes. She sat straight, her hands carefully placed on top of her stylish silver-clasped purse. Her features were pointed but soft. She looked very confident and sure, like a schoolteacher or secretary, Kimberlane thought.

The tattered pale blonde, who looked unable to speak above a dove's peak, stared at the stately Negro woman and roared, "You expect me to sit there next to her?" The conductor froze as everyone turned to see who was causing the commotion. The woman, who now swayed recklessly as the train pulled to a sudden start, squealed, "I'll sit there!" She whirled, pointing wildly at the empty seat next to Kimberlane. The funny man sitting across from Kimberlane covered his mouth with his broad hand and started to giggle.

It took Kimberlane several more stops to figure out what was funny. When she did, she laughed straight out loud, while slapping the little blonde's bony thigh.

5

Family? What Family?

THE WALK DOWN MEMORY LANE proved that some things were changed and some things were definitely the same. Yesterday, when she had been able to tear herself away from the enthralling conversation about her worthiness as an object of the two men's attention, she eventually made her way to her old apartment. It was the one she had shared with Aunt Mattie and Uncle E. She walked right up to the vanilla-colored brick building. It stood alone; two vacant lots bordered it. A piece of paper here and a tin can there, clanging against the concrete, gave it a lonely feeling. The vestibule now sported a lock, which meant she could not get in to knock on the interior door. Fortunately, the apartment she had lived in was on the ground floor so she tapped on the window, five times hard.

"Who is it?" The growl came as the window screeched open.

"Er, it's uh…I used to live here. Can I please talk to you?"

"You'd better not be selling anything." The rotund woman belted as she slammed the window shut. A few minutes later she emerged from the entryway, pulling one small child by each hand. "Well, whata ya want?" she spat.

"Have you lived here long?"

"Long enough. Listen, I don't know if I wasn't plain enough for you, but if I don't want to buy anything I sure don't want to be doing no survey. If you got a point—"

"Mattie and E Smith, do you know them?"

The boys ran to Kimberlane's skirt-tail and the giant beige woman shrank to human-size. "Come in, sweetie. What's your name?"

Kimberlane left 2012 Oak Drive a bit smaller herself. Finding out that Mattie had passed away was both bitter and painful, but at least this aunt had a reason for leaving her. Carolyn Bosh sat her down on a worn armchair, gave her apple pie and milk, and explained that Mattie had watched her boys for an entire week when she had to travel south to tend her mother. She also said that Mattie had taken in kids for years, probably because her own child died at birth. Kimberlane thought of how the lumps of sweet-tasting apple soured and got caught in her throat when she heard this. Must run in the family, she fretted. Mattie lost a baby and compensated by taking in other people's children. Why hadn't she ever told her? They could have comforted each other.

In her heart, Kimberlane knew Mattie had to be

dead. It gave her a strange comfort when Mrs. Bosh confirmed her suspicion. To know that her auntie had not completely abandoned her by choice felt good.

So much for family reunions, Kimberlane mused as she slumped down the stairs that led away from 2012 Oak Drive.

ॐ

"Ashes to ashes, dust to dust," Kimberlane heard from the graveyard as she pressed her way toward the cemetery. Couldn't the ministers ever think of anything unusual or original to say? It was a sad alternative, but perhaps she could visit Mattie here. Rabid winds threatened to rip the pillbox hat off her head while pulling the uncovered strands of her hair from its pins. Leaves and debris whirled around her. Kimberlane Steel's high-heeled shoes dug miniature trenches in the moist dirt, and she felt as if she was sinking backward in every way that mattered.

Her grandfather, Edward Steel of Steel and Son Corporation, had sent her home. There was a sense of urgency in his "request" and he had barely given her time to pack, saying she needed to get going the next day. Both her mother's and father's families had apparently compared notes on the best way to get rid of an unwanted member: DO IT FAST. Edward had given her money, but how long would it last, and would there be more? So many questions.

The clouds, that had been high and wispy, rose and roiled fast into the distance as bulbous deep purple bullies muscled them out. Kimberlane carefully opened her plaid umbrella.

"Let go!" she yelled immediately, fighting the fiendish wind for control. In spite of the signs, no rain descended, only sorrow. In a casket somewhere out there lay Mattie, her mother's only sister, cold and silent. Some things never changed. Such a solitary woman. Not many people would have attended her service. There would be the minister in his slate-gray robe and Uncle E, his back a little rounder and his head more bald than when she left years ago. So sad that her close-knit family had unraveled. To think that she had to learn Mattie and E's fate from a stranger upon her return home to Chicago.

"Hello, dear, you have someone buried here, too?" a calming voice spoke. The older woman who possessed it sauntered out from behind heavy shrubs pulling the collar of her caped coat over her chest.

"I'm not sure," Kimberlane sighed. "My aunt may be buried here."

"Why don't you take a look, or better still, come back tomorrow when the proprietor is in. He'll be able to tell you just where your loved one is. What's the name?"

"Her formal name was Martine."

"Martine…hummm."

"What's your name, ma'am?"

"My formal name is Roseland. People around here call me Mama Rose."

"Mama Rose." Kimberlane's glance jumped side to side; tombstones jutted forward to surround her.

"I, uh, I'll see you later, Miss Rose. Very nice to meet you. Have a nice day."

Kimberlane whipped around, her steps racing back over the rickety moss-covered cobblestone path she had inadvertently taken to the cemetery entrance. The cemetery, the place of withered dreams and lost hopes; lots of people with no place to go and in no hurry to get there. Just like her.

Fumbling hands dried tears now rushing from her treacherous eyes. Poor Mattie. Kimberlane wondered if her real family was here in this cemetery or was it the walking dead she'd left back in Pennsylvania. She never imagined she'd be back in her old South Side neighborhood. There were fewer houses with their distinctive porches and varied windows. There were too many liquor stores and a great many apartment buildings. Apparently many of the whites had moved out, since she had seen more black people already than she had in all the time she had resided here; it seemed so many years ago. So what: the neighborhood had changed. She had started out one way and ended totally different herself. Life had been cruel to her, crueler than to most, she suspected. At the end of her high school freshman year she had been banished to an existence so unreal that it could only occur in a mystery novel. She didn't announce her return and she doubted at age twenty-seven anyone would recognize her. She was different in ways that would doubtless baffle many and wound others. It was decided then, she would remain incognito until she had some idea how people would react to her.

Swish…the rustling of budding life announced people approaching through the prickly emerald covering. Suddenly nervous, Kimberlane dropped behind the smooth stone of an enormous obelisk. Hunched, her cheek hugging its slick surface, she read: With love and dedication to our sister May Wright. The towering lettering, a sure pretense; a family compensating for things they should have done while May Wright walked the earth. No matter, the guilt of May's family had provided Kimberlane with the perfect hiding place.

A springy little girl bounced and swayed toward her as an adorable sandy-haired boy tried snagging her ponytail. Catching the hem of her bright orange dress, he tumbled to the ground. They rolled head over feet down a little bump.

A cinnamon-colored woman walking as if each foot was being pulled from its own personal swamp, lagged wearily behind. Her words were purposeful. "Up!" she roared, grabbing the boy by his collar and yanking him off the ground. "Now listen, we're only here for a minute; pay your respects and let's get going," she yelped. "And, Charlie, tell Jennifer you're sorry."

'Charlie': what a nice name and what a cute little boy…her own child would have…Kimberlane caught herself—what good did it do to think about it? She had done what she had done. At the time it seemed right; thinking of it now, well, she'd rather die.

Kimberlane watched as they continued their stroll and chase. It was impossible to tell whom they were there to visit. Wait a minute, is that…it is.

"There's my boy!" James came up behind Charlie and hefted him into the air. He patted the girl on her head.

So he has a son. For some reason that thought bothered Kimberlane. And they don't look a thing alike. Suddenly something about the boy's appearance unsettled her. There were too many ghosts here; perhaps just this one time she should have disobeyed her grandfather and bypassed Chicago altogether.

6

❧

I Know You

SITTING AT THE BRIGHTLY LIT Woolworth lunch counter drumming her fingers, Kimberlane eyed the metal coffee pot. Steaming condensation gathered on its surface. Miss Mims, the fifty-something waitress with thin pink lips and big blond flip, which would have been questionable on a women ten years her junior, was asking to take her order for the second time. Again she said, "I'll have coffee, plain black coffee, please."

"Oh yeah, I got that," Miss Mims said, yelling the request over the cook counter when the pot was sitting inches from her grasp.

Kimberlane was removing her feet from the rest and turning on the high metal stool when Mike came up and sat next to her. He had been clumsy and shy as a young man. He was now handsome, but he had a tendency toward being overweight—she knew about those things.

"Hello again, Miss, er…?" Mike's voice trailed off.

"I didn't give my name before."

"But you do have one." He offered his broad hand.

"Indeed." She smiled, "Steel; Kimberlane Steel," she offered her now thin, perfectly manicured hand. My, how things had changed.

"You seem familiar to me," he said taking her hand in his, "I just can't figure where I know you from."

"Give it time. It'll come to you."

"I'm Michael Swane. Is Chicago your home?" He bowed his big redhead slightly, demonstrating that not all of his shyness had dissipated since 1957, the year of her demise and rebirth, so to speak.

"Home," she mused, looking around the now crowded store. Women were holding the arms of their men and little boys scampered about their mother's skirt-hems. Little girls twirled their curls and pigtails. Miss Mims had become a great deal more efficient due to the hurried pace. Blueberry tarts and apple pies flew from the cook counter to the customer counter, receipts were written in short hand and both she and Mike had coffee refills without a single request. "Home," she repeated. "I hardly know what that means."

"You're a mysterious woman," Mike said as he removed an enormous red berry muffin from the Servelle and took a generous chump.

"You don't know the half of it," she said eyeing the crumbs on his lip, "but I don't like to talk about me. What about you? What does Mike Swane do?"

"Mike Swane is not a mystery at all. Sorry," he continued, taking another enormous bite and wiping the morsels from his lip with the back of his free hand, "do you want a piece?"

She shook her head.

"I work, pray and live within a ten-block radius of this place right here," he pointed down as if home was the Woolworth store. "When my family moved here it was all white, lots of Jews. Then, it was a little bit of everybody; mostly white. Now it's a little bit of everybody, mostly black."

"Does that bother you?"

"Huh?"

"That it's mostly black, does it bother you?" She questioned.

"Does it bother you?" Mike leaned and looked intently into her eyes; it made her fidget and gave her a queasy feeling.

"Me?" she asked, a little too wide-eyed, "you think...ur...no, it doesn't bother me at all. I think God created all people equal and the people who don't know that ought to be cut off altogether, like the prophet David said in one of the scriptures."

"That's cute. I haven't heard David referred to as a prophet," Mike responded, grinning big.

"You think I'm ignorant, don't you?"

"No, just cute." His cocked brow flitted.

"Well, what about you? Are you a bigot?"

"Me, heck no. My best friend is Negro. You saw him, tall, dark and solemn." He made a large grab past her to the sugar packets, "Now what's that smile about?"

"Just thinking. Mike, do you know any nice places to stay in this area? I've been staying at the Southton Hotel."

"Wow, you're living there...on Parpell Avenue?

Lady, you must be in the dough."

"Yes, no." She replied as he raised his skeptical brow and lowered his coffee cup. He then made an all too apparent head-to-toe scan of her person. "That's rude."

"What?"

"Do you always ogle new acquaintances so shamelessly?"

"That obvious, am I? It's just that...well, like I said, you're a mystery, eating at Woolworth and staying at the Southton. I once wandered up into that place with those golden high-beam ceilings and silver-threaded majestic carpets and thought I had accidentally come into an ancient Egyptian palace."

Kimberlane nearly spewed her coffee listening to his blatant exaggeration, "Mike, you're a card. Anyway, do you know of a place or not? Despite your hasty assessment of me, I'm not picky."

"Then I may be able to help you even if you are a little picky." His head was cocked, his grin playful. "There are some apartments available in a beautiful court-way building a couple of streets over from where I live."

"Why, Mr. Swane, you wouldn't be trying to keep me at arm's length, would you?"

"Would you object if I was?"

"It depends; are you dangerous?"

"Only if you count being obvious. Listen, these apartments are really nice and my bud—"

"You don't have to convince me; can I move in today?"

"The owner's out of town but if you trust me I can help you move some stuff in later tonight. You can meet him tomorrow. Is your face always so expressive?" He stared directly at her, "Don't worry—he trusts me and you can, too."

"Nev—"

"Huh?"

"Never mind meeting the owner. What are you doing now?"

"Nothing, if I can be instrumental in making you my neighbor."

"Would you settle for showing me the place so I can see if your evaluation is accurate?"

"Lady, you've got a date."

The brick court-way building was beautifully situated. The grounds on either side of the walkway between the tiers that faced each other were impeccably maintained. Plush grass lined carefully manicured shrubs. There was not a nick in the cement, not a weed between the cracks. The windows were sparkling clean and that was just the outside. Looking at the handsome state of the place, Kimberlane couldn't imagine why all the apartments weren't taken.

"A penny for your thoughts," Mike sliced through the blinding sunlight. "It's nice, isn't it? This is a new purchase. The whole building has been refurbished and the deadbeat tenants ousted."

"You mean the landlord put people out who couldn't pay?"

"He wouldn't consider that deadbeat. He put the people out who should be able to pay but refuse to put in the effort. He's a fair man."

Kimberlane smirked then squinted into the sun. "Isn't that the man you were with the other day? And who's that little boy with him?" She noted the fair-skinned boy from the cemetery. He had a lanky build and sad shoulders. Something about him gave her the shudders.

"Yes, that's James and the little boy's Charlie."

"His son?"

"A kind of godson you might say. Full name's Charlie Drake. I didn't know the family; they had some misfortune and couldn't care for the boy. Mrs. Timmons took him in, a kind of unofficial foster care; but she's thinking of putting him into the system. She's got five of her own. I think James would adopt him if he had a woman." Mike turned to call out to Charlie.

"So he's never been married then…" Kimberlane blinked and shook her head.

"What was that?" Mike giggled as Charlie came running.

"He looks very sad, Mike." She pulled a handkerchief from her purse and dabbed the moisture threatening her eyes.

"Who, James?"

"Him, too." She mumbled, fluttering to clear her vision to get a better look at the boy who was impossibly familiar.

"You really have a way with kids." James huffed having run to catch up with Charlie.

Kimberlane was only vaguely aware of the raw energy that hovered above her, only mildly interested in the scent of him standing near. She was lost in the moment, enamored and curiously drawn to the handsome young boy who invited her with his eyes to a hug.

"By now he should be wriggling free." James continued looming tall and blocking all of the sunlight. "He usually doesn't take to people so freely." He stood protectively. "What is it about you?"

"Kindred spirits," Kimberlane blinked from her bowed posture, "I can feel he's had a loss or two."

A warring-smirk battled on James' lips. Was he amused or annoyed? He looked to Mike for an explanation. Mike sensing his friend's lack of ease quickly supplied, "I told her about Charlie's family."

"Why, you're charming all of the South Side, aren't you? Mike doesn't usually open up so freely either."

"You sound sorta jealous, buddy," Mike quipped. "Kimberlane has a way with people and men in particular. Charlie here is no exception. Are you, boy?" he ruffled the child's hair. Charlie smiled, then ran off to play with some boys rounding the corner.

"I'm just saying I've never seen him take to a stranger like that." James winced causing his cheek to quiver.

"It's odd, seems like I know him." Kimberlane puzzled, getting to her feet and dusting off her platinum-colored hose.

"Well, don't get attached," James pronounced. "Enjoy your date," he finished bluntly, following the same path Charlie had taken.

❧

"Hold up there, Charlie!" Yesterday James had returned a day early from a business trip and gone right to pick Charlie up. He was shocked to see Mike with that woman they had seen near the Southton. Mike was nothing if not slow and deliberate. To move this fast on anything was way out of his character. And the way Charlie took to the woman…odd. Anyway, today his focus was his unofficial godson.

Carla had given hint after hint that it wouldn't be long before she turned Charlie over to the authorities for adoption, foster care or whatever the state could do. "I just can't keep up, Mr. James; I can barely care for my own."

"If it's about money…" he had ventured.

"It's not just that. I'm an old woman. I don't have the strength."

James gritted his teeth and walked away. He didn't blame her really. He was young and healthy and he couldn't see how he could manage to raise a young boy on his own. So days like today were his way of saying, "I care and goodbye."

Fun Town was Charlie's favorite place in the 'whole wide world' as he was fond of saying, and now he was hurling toward the Himalayan Express roller coaster at rocket speed.

"What?" Charlie yelled back to James' nearly forgotten exclamation. He was not looking where he was running.

"I said, 'wait for me.' What's your rush? We've got all day." James broke into a jog himself.

Strange, James thought as a flash of recognition came and went. He was passing the woman who was popping up daily now.

"Hey, buddy," his friend bellowed as he came to an abrupt stop. "Kimberlane and I were taking a walk when she thought about Funtown. She wanted to come and see if the place was all she had heard, so we grabbed a bus and hustled over here."

"Just like that?"

"Spontaneous; she's kinda got that effect."

"I see..." He really didn't. Mike wasn't acting himself. He was a workhorse, never really took spontaneous breaks. For that matter James could have been referring to himself; it was one of the things they had in common...yet they were both at Funtown having uncharacteristic fun.

"You know, Mike, I haven't formally met your lady."

"Whoa, James, you have—?"

"Mr. James," she extended her hand, "my name is Kimberlane." James looked past her, checking to see that Charlie was okay. He'd found a friend.

"Hummm..." James mused.

"Sorry, good people; manners missing again," Mike piped up. "Miss Kimberlane Steel, James Johnson."

James finally noticed her outstretched hand, "I'm sorry, Miss Steel." James took her soft hand in his, "Anybody ever call you —?"

"No; not anymore, I prefer Kimberlane."

"Sorry...I was just thinking...so, you're not married?" He was staring at her other hand.

"James, man, you having an off day? That's fairly

personal."

"It is...don't know what's come over me." He dropped her hand. "I was just thinking how good you were with Charlie yesterday. I bet you have a way with all kids. Well, Mike must be pleased."

"Humm?"

"Seems you'll make some man a good wife."

"Thank you, I think."

"I, uggh...I didn't mean...I'm sorry...this is personal stuff and not like me. Uhh...forgive me...err...so what were you two doing by the building?"

"Doing..."

"Yesterday. Did Mike tell you how we started our business? How we get them?"

"Get them...?"

"Yeah, he's told a few people. People he trusts and since you two seem to be getting to know each other so quickly..."

"Mr. Johnson, we seem to be missing each other in this conversation. I was at that building looking it over. I was hoping to rent there. We're going to meet the landlord when we leave here. Mike tells me he's a real workaholic. Mike says he's probably there right now."

"He did, did he?" James laughed.

"Yes, and that's not all; I guess he's a fairly hard man."

"Is that so?"

"Ahem, Kimberlane." Mike coughed into his fist and pulled lightly at her elbow.

"Hard, but perhaps fair?" she said over her shoulder.

"I hope so." James squared his jaw and raised a brow.

"What's it to you?"

"I'm the landlord."

It took Kimberlane a minute to get over her chagrin. Had she been in Pennsylvania so long that she had forgotten the accomplishments of colored people?

"What did you think?" James questioned defiantly.

"I...I like the outside and I'm looking forward to knowing the...the...inside," she stuttered.

James furrowed his brow as little Charlie came running past him and Mike to hug the skirt tail of the woman everyone seemed hell-bent on loving.

Later that day, Mike dropped Kimberlane off at James' building and promised to come back as soon as he was done checking on his father who had been under the weather. "You'll be safe with him," he joked as he walked away. "He's usually not this odd. I think Charlie's leaving has got him a little shaken up."

Kimberlane smiled when she saw James and Charlie standing straight and formal at the entryway of the front-facing building, which was flanked by the two that faced each other forming a U-shaped trio. She was surprised when both James and Charlie offered their arms as she arrived at the door. She decided to take the little man's. James shook his head as if he wondered what he had just been thinking and doing.

They walked up the clean wooden stairwell, down the carpeted second-floor hall and into a nice quaint apartment. She knew she'd be taking it because little Charlie Drake looked up at her with his puppy eyes and announced, "Mr. James and me painted it together. I'm glad he let me help with the color. It's right for you." James appeared to be shaking his head but she wasn't paying much attention to him. She felt a literal heart-tug when she thought of Charlie's child hands stirring the paint, mixing the color. Anyway, it just felt right.

Charlie was telling her how much fun he and Mr. James had this morning. He wanted to know why she and Mike didn't want to stay and play with them. Kimberlane's admiration for James was growing. It was a real testament to this single man. He owned property and seemed to have many responsibilities, yet he took out time to educate and train a boy in need, not only of a family but of someone to teach him to be a man.

The living room was painted creamy beige, with one bedroom off to the left. The kitchen and small dining area were combined and located to the right. She had to search for the small bath, which was fortunately near her room. When she was a child the bathroom was down the hall and shared by another family and when she was a teen the bathrooms were seemingly too numerous to count. Life was funny; best to be grateful for what you had when you had it.

"I like it very much," she said, walking toward

the large glass doors.

"If you decide to take it, I'll unseal those. The last tenants had a little girl and they worried about her falling. It's a pretty view of the courtyard even though we're just on the second story. The rent is due on the first of the month with no exceptions. Will that work with your pay schedule?" He moved to her side and parted the curtains. Their arms were touching.

"I hardly see what difference my pay schedule makes," her voice trembled, "since you have declared that there are no exceptions."

"I can't argue with that logic—the first it is."

"Careful, Kimberlane," they both jumped, "or you're liable to get his higher rate," Mike chimed from the apartment doorway as James released the curtain.

"Yes, I usually charge two: one for whites and a lower for blacks."

"Why do you do that? It must break some kind of law. You could get in trouble."

"You sound concerned." The tilt of his mouth had the most subtle hint of sensuality.

"I'm not. I don't even know you—"

"Don't worry, I won't charge you the higher rate."

"You, you won't…"

"You're Mike's friend. Therefore, unless you do something to prove otherwise, you're my friend; and I break rules for my friends all the time. That's why I was asking you about your pay schedule."

"Oh, I'm your friend now?"

"Can you be my friend, too?" Charlie's bright eyes and small hand winging the hem of her skirt, like the little boys in the Woolworth store, caused her to swallow loudly.

She turned her attention to the neatly dressed boy, "Well, of course, I'll be your friend." She leaned to pinch his cheek. Her hand lingered as she allowed the back of her fingertips to glide to his chin, "I haven't made up my mind about Mr. Johnson and his two rates."

"Mr. James is a good man, and anyway, you need him."

"What?" James and Kimberlane howled together.

"You don't have a place to stay or a family," James and Mike were giving Charlie squints and scowls, "do you?"

"Well, no, not really."

"Then you need us." God, he looked like he meant what he was saying. Had he grown up without the love he needed? Kimberlane sure hoped James Johnson really was worthy of the love this little boy was giving him.

"I'll take it, and don't worry—my employer pays in time to get the rent by the first."

7

❧

A Tale of Two Aunts

JAMES FELT LIKE he was in a twisted version of a fairytale. His: the Prince and Tin Can of Peas. He could hear every squeak of the coils in his mattress and he couldn't seem to pound the lumps out of his pillow. He twisted right then left. Kicking the annoyingly crisp sheets from his legs, he bounded from bed. He had hardly slept but could not tolerate lying flat another minute. The light of day prodded: do something. Three doors down and a million miles away she lay and for some reason he could barely wait to see how Miss Steel was adjusting to her new accommodations. An entire week had passed and he had not made his 'friendly manager' visit.

He rapped on the door three times. He could hear her scurrying to answer it.

"Mr. Johnson?" she rasped, pushing at the edges of her hair while pulling bobby pins from her pouty mouth. "Is there something wrong?" She managed through clenched teeth.

He remembered how he'd left her that first night.

"Very good, Miss Steel," he'd launched, "I'm sure you'll like it here. If you need anything just let Mike know; he handles most of the maintenance." Arrogant. Why couldn't he resort to something other than cool, calm and unconcerned when he was nervous? And why did she make him nervous? She had screwed her face into squinted eyes and cheeks full of air. A human question mark.

He turned and left, literally scratching his head as he did.

He'd get it right today. This visit would vindicate him and assure her that he was indeed a levelheaded man simply doing his job.

"Tell me about your family." He heard himself blurt to her question.

"What an interesting salutation, Mr. Johnson. Do you greet all of your new tenants this way?"

"No, I'm not sure what I was thinking. Was your door locked, because I didn't hear the lock tumble before you opened it?"

"No, it wasn't. I didn't just get up. I've been out already. Isn't there a security lock on the ground floor?"

"Yes, but you can't trust that. Kids sometimes prop the door so they can run in and out."

"You're worried about me."

Say something smart, James, "You are Mike and Charlie's...er investment and..."

"Investment. That doesn't sound very kind, a person being an investment. Do they get a cut of my rent?"

"Well, yes. I mean, no. Charlie doesn't...he's just...Can we start over?"

"You mean like my move-in day when you declared that I'd like it fine here or this pleasant visit starting with a demand that I tell you about my family?"

James shook his head and felt suddenly ridiculous. "Miss Steel," he said placing both hands on her shoulders, "I'm not sure why, but you make me a little nervous."

"I do?" She smiled, "Good." Kimberlane freed herself from his grip and motioned for him to be seated at her small dining room table. "Thank you for coming to check on me."

"It's no problem. I only live...is that weak tea?"

"What?"

"The tea, it's mostly milk and I bet sugar."

"Yes, it is. My aunt used to make it this way." Her head tilted slightly toward the ceiling.

"A pleasant thought?"

"Yes." She danced around the table placing a napkin she pulled from a brown shopping bag on his knee before placing one on her own lap and pushing the cup of tea in his direction. "So what is it, Mr. Johnson, did you come all this way to censure me about my lax security or did you really want to know about my family?"

After taking a sip of the tea and wishing he had waited for it to cool off, he tried to be more relaxed. "I came to check on you."

"Really." Kimberlane rested her head on her braided fingers allowing her sooty cocoa lashes to flutter charmingly. James could feel himself being lulled.

"Yes, I like to know a little something about the

people who live in my buildings."

"Oh," she snapped, "if that's all, I can assure you I'm safe." She snatched the delicate yellow teacup from his suspended hand.

"Wait. Tell me about your family. I'm interested, really."

The question mark face came back and so did the tea. She took a deep breath and sat down again.

"I think I'll start with my two aunts: Aunt Mattie, as we called her at home, was a tall slender woman." She looked up as if struggling to remember, "Mattie worked super hard and seemed to be grumpy most of the time because of it. When she wasn't taking care of her sick husband, she was ordering me out of her kitchen. I had a bit of a problem back then."

"You didn't like her cooking?"

"You are very kind, Mr. Johnson; I liked it too much. Anyway, she saved most of her tenderness for my uncle. She also had a son who was grown and gone. I never knew him and she rarely spoke about him. His name was Phillip."

"You came here for her funeral, Mike said." Kimberlane twisted in her chair and ever so carefully rung her hands. For a few moments there was silence and James suddenly became aware that he had perhaps given too much leeway to his young apprentice. The boy thought he was an artist and had asked if he could do some mixing with the paint. James hadn't paid much attention until now. The pink and purple undertones of the kitchen paint leaped at him, taunting, *We have a secret and we're going to tell.* "What do you think of Charlie's paint job?" he ventured, cutting off his own line of questioning.

"It's charming. Dull colorless walls have never thrilled me but walls shouldn't be too bold. You and Charlie struck a good balance."

The walls were calmer now and James enjoyed his tea much better. "I interrupted you—you were saying?"

"I was saying that I did come here because my aunt passed. I think...er...let's talk about my other aunt: Eleanor. She is a little woman and like my aunt Mattie—though they were not related—talked about my weight quite a bit. Besides that, her favorite topics included my hair, my manners and my inability to enunciate with pristine definition, as she put it."

"If it's any consolation, I think you talk just fine." James knew he was staring at her but he couldn't help it. He was feeling agitated; who were these people who could only find fault?

"Why, thank you, Mr. Johnson," she said gratefully, her sparkling eyes dancing.

"You're welcome, Miss Steel." Driven to relieve his curiosity, he questioned, "Is that it? Is that your whole family?"

"I have a grandfather; it was really he who sent me here."

"What's he like?"

"Tall, affluent, slender, demanding, aloof, influential, austere—"

"Hold on there, you're talking to a man with two years of junior college under his belt. I got most of that but you might want to break it down a bit."

"Why do you do that, James? You know exactly what I'm saying. You've always been very intelligent."

"Miss Steel, I appreciate the compliment but you

talk as if you know me."

"I don't!" The table rattled as she nervously kicked the leg. "Do you want to hear about my grandfather or not."

"Sure," James said, thinking Kimberlane was one of the strangest women he had met.

"Well, he demanded that I be brought to him when I was a child. I stayed until I was as you see me now and he demanded that I leave."

"Just like that?"

"Just like that." She snapped her finger.

"The people in your world seem kinda…"

"Cold…I'd say that about sums them up."

"Didn't you have anyone who…"

"Who loved me? I thought I did, once…"

"Sounds like a man. You sure you want to talk about it?"

"No, actually I don't. But it's not as bad as I make it out to be. I believe Grandfather, Aunt Eleanor and Aunt Mattie, especially Aunt Mattie, loved me in their own way; and they're all I've ever known."

James felt sorry for this poor lonely woman. She was such a quandary. Why had she come to this neighborhood, when judging by her clothes and manners she could live anywhere in Chicago? There were only a few whites still living in his court-way building but she insisted on staying there and had paid him four months in advance on the rent. She said his friend Mike had told her he was the best landlord in the neighborhood. And while he knew that was true, people of her means usually chose to live in the white-run apartment buildings.

"And what about you, Mr. Johnson…" She reeled on him looking innocent and mischievous at the same time, "What's your story?"

"Story," James jumped to his feet, "I don't have any story."

Such a curious man, that James Johnson. Kimberlane winced pulling bobby pins from her tight bun and letting herself experience the freedom of the waves about her face. All day long she had thought about James' morning visit. He seemed so sympathetic, so kind, so…human. Shaking her head from side to side she peered at her reflection as layer upon layer of mahogany fluff settled on her shoulders. She pulled her hands through the tangled mass. Truth be told, she liked her hair, but without her people here to do it, well, she'd rather just keep it pinned up.

So James didn't have a story and she wished to God she could forget hers. Memories came often, unannounced and unwanted.

If only she could forget. Kimberlane plopped down in the middle of her bedroom floor pulling her pilfered covers and pillows from the Southton over her legs and shoulders. She was trying desperately to dispel the ghosts of her past as she drifted into an uneasy sleep.

"Destination Philly!" The conductor shouted as she disembarked that train. Her mouth went dry and her eyes welled wet as she entered the gray of the station building. What had she done at the age of fifteen to be banished from Aunt Mattie and Uncle E's home? A howling "why" ran up the

walls to the height of the ceiling and bound down so hard it threatened to crush her. Her left arm stretched from its socket. The light green Samsonite which teetered from her fingers was stuffed to the point of bursting. She had tried to put every item she owned in it fearing that if she left even the smallest thing she would have no way to recall who she really was. The latch on her purse-full-of-nothing was easing its way open just as her lips parted to let loose that yell.

"Kimberlane Smith!" she heard a royal voice command. Her head snapped up and she saw the sign: Kimberlane Smith-Steel. It was written bold and fancy. Desperately she rushed toward the richly dressed man holding it.

"Are you related to my mother?" Her voice was shaky and frantic.

"Miss Steel, I presume?"

"Humm, what?" She looked over her shoulder.

"I'm sorry, you must be Miss Smith," he corrected.

It took Kimberlane a minute to figure out what the proper man with the strange way of speaking was trying to say. He was talking to her but why did he call her Steel at first. Her last name was Smith, although a "Miss Smith" she had never been."

"I'm Kimberlane,." she stated flatly.

"And I'm Joseph. Our car is over there, miss." With that he leaned, pulled her bag from her hand and headed off. She followed.

They walked past five or six dark cars and a spiffy sky-blue one. Kimberlane's Chicago family had never owned a car and when they reached a rather shabby grey vehicle she figured they had arrived. "No, Miss Kimberlane." Joseph stopped, squared his shoulders and pointed with his free hand, "Further this way."

Her eyes nearly popped their sockets. She stood in front of a powdery tan car with glossy silver polished trim along the sides, around the fish-eyed headlights, and smack down the center of the hood. The tires had huge moon-shaped silver rims encircled by wide white bands, which didn't sport a speck of dust or dirt anywhere. The word "Buick" served as its nose and the front grill, which resembled shark's teeth, gritting a warning, "I'll swallow you whole if you don't quit pretendin' and get back on that train."

"This can't be right!" Kimberlane panicked. "I don't know anybody who lives like this. Please can I just go home?"

"Don't be afraid, Miss Steel, you are home. Your family is waiting for you."

"My family, my family!?"

Kimberlane twisted violently. She hadn't yelled out…had she? She wasn't fifteen, she wasn't in a train station in Philadelphia, nor was she in her Pennsylvania home. She was in her very first apartment and God forbid she should start having her howling-mares, as her aunt Eleanor called them. It was just about worth going through the torment of having those dreams when Kimberlane remembered waking to the sight of Eleanor's heavy auburn hair hanging restlessly from her pale sleep bonnet and over the dark rings beneath her eyes. Eleanor would try to shake her awake while simultaneously attempting to cover her ears. "Must I always be the one to wake you?" she'd rant, filling Kimberlane's cavernous room with her high pitch and the smell of faint roses. "Am I the one who caused you to have these demented dreams?" Kimberlane had wanted to slap her hard every time that absurd phrase escaped her tiny mouth. She had never suffered nightmares until she suffered Eleanor's atrocities. She often wondered who Eleanor tormented before she came along.

"Enough!" Kimberlane shushed herself, "I want to live here and now." James had no story and hers was horrifying. She pulled her sheets around her hips, cocooned herself in woolen blankets and piled her three pillows high while wondering if the fifty dollar bill she had laid on the bare hotel mattresses made up for her crime. Easier to do and then make amends: her grandfather's words buzzed her ears like nagging gnats. The sound was so vivid that she looked around half-thinking to see him. She thought about her new place: this apartment. It would do. It was clean and large enough. Besides this bedroom, she had a small kitchenette and dining area and there was a full living room with a balcony overlooking a beautifully polished courtyard. Thoughts of her new life and new people collided with the old she'd left behind. Together they rocked her to an uneasy sleep.

With woozy wakefulness, Kimberlane attempted to rouse herself. Who had taken her sumptuous four-poster bed and replaced it with this bed of nails? She rolled over to reach for the servant chime. Somebody was going to pay. Instead of the nightstand her arm flopped to the ground and slowly her situation dawned on her. She was sleeping on hard floor. Unfortunately for her, the soft cushion of thick covers was wrestled from its place by her twisting and squirming. She should have known: a calm sleeper she had never been.

So what should a woman of leisure with a decent sum of money, which may or may not be replenished, do with herself on the second week of occupying her new apartment? Go furniture shopping, of course. A few modest pieces wouldn't put too much of a strain on her finances. Then next week she'd look for gainful employment. "Put your hands to the plow," her grandfather would say on many occasions, though Kimberlane had never seen him do it himself. Kimberlane pushed away her covers and ran from her room; she'd go out onto the balcony to test the weather. Locked. Sealed shut. James had said he'd unseal them and he didn't seem the type to dawdle. She wondered why he hadn't done what he promised or for that matter ever come again to see how she was settling in. While simmering over her fate she noticed that the clouds and wind outside were doing some simmering of their own.

Hat, trench coat, umbrella...but she'd wear that cute little blue number underneath. She wouldn't wait another day to wear it. After all, it had taken her a few extra weeks to be able to shimmy into it.

"What am I gonna do? What skills do I have?" Kimberlane said to no one in particular. She had paid James four months in advance; he wouldn't hear of charging her a security deposit, said any friend of Mike's could be trusted. The truth was, in his mind he had only just met her when Mike did and that was less than three weeks ago. So why this trust, this gallantry? Perhaps he really did trust Mike's judgment but why did Mike trust her? She'd have to ask him. So where to start? She needed an income if for no other reason than to explain how she sustained herself. Since Mike was her 'friend' now, why not ask him. It was Saturday and the Woolworth counter had proved a favorite of his on at least two Saturdays in a row. Let's just see if he was a true creature of habit.

Kimberlane walked into the store. The bright lights were a welcome contrast to the dank dreariness of the outside. Nine o'clock in the morning and it looked like midnight, the clouds were black and threatening. Few souls had been brave enough to venture out but sure as you bet there he sat. His large red head was leaned over a steaming cup of coffee, water dripping from his hair and face. Miss Mims was behind the counter. Her lips were cherry red today and her hair, minus the flip, hung to her shoulders. She sported a short-sleeved shirt, skin hanging from her elbows like a chicken's neck. Kimberlane had a strange urge to crow but instead let out an over enthusiastic, "Howdy, Mike." Mike looked stunned at first and then pleased.

"Have a seat, Kimberlane."

"So, Mike, do you come here often?"

"Every Saturday like clockwork."

Miss Mims snorted as she came by to refresh his cup, "I don't know what line he's feedin' ya, honey, but I've worked this morning shift for five years and if I've seen this fella' five times, three have been in the last three weeks."

"Ah, don't listen to Sandi—"

"Shirley, see," Miss Mims said plunking the pot down on the counter and pointing to her nametag.

"Okay, I give. I came here hoping to see you."

"That's very sweet, Mike. You are a very nice man," she said as she removed her coat and laid it on the seat next to her. Mike was a big man and by the time she realized he was getting up from his stool to assist her she was already seated next to him.

"Mike, I need a job, a profession. What needs doing around here?"

"Humm, I don't know about close around but Bilco, downtown, is looking for some line workers for their new factory. And oh yeah, that new club is looking for a coat check girl."

Apparently noticing her grimace, he became more thoughtful and creative. "And the after school program, I don't know how long they're gonna last. Rumor is they're having some financial problems but...I think they're looking for someone to keep it going in the meantime. Lots of the neighborhood kids use the program. With all this talk of teacher strikes, they might even need you in the day. Got any skills?"

"Why...yes," she said with some hesitation. "Okay, no," she admitted, "but I'm a very quick learner and when I want something I go after it."

Kimberlane lay with her hands resting under her head on her big stuffed pillow in her new apartment. Two great things had happened: one, the center had said she could come for an interview when their supervisor was back from vacation, and two, her new bed had arrived. She called home and before she could even tell Joseph what she wanted, he promised he'd personally make sure she had a bed that reminded her of home within a week. It was extravagant and didn't match any of the meager furnishings she'd gathered since living here; so what! A little piece of the Pennsylvania life cradled her body like the arms of a strong man, something—come to think of it—she had never really experienced. She tossed under the rich feel of her sumptuous new sheets and covers and let her mattress swallow her. She drifted off into a radiant sleep. Tomorrow she'd go do battle for a job she was not qualified to have. When had that ever stopped her?

✎

The room was cold, the people colder. Her aunt loomed near while the stabbing in her stomach slashed over and over again. She felt sick and weak. "What's wrong with me, Aunt Eleanor?"

"Now you've done it, Kimberlane, it's always about you. Take this medicine!" She remembered looking into her aunt's wild eyes. "It's best for everyone. If Ashton knew…no, he'd never accept you or this…"

"But what's wrong with me, Auntie?"

"Kimberlane, you can't be this naïve…you really don't know, do you? It's like this…" The room went dark and began to spin. The pain became unbearable. Then there was blackness, bleak and complete. Suddenly her belly was still, the room was still and life had ceased forever done, forever gone.

You did it. It's all your fault. You're weak, too weak, not good enough, not ever good enough. The hound barked at her and pounced; it was snarling and foaming, its razor-sharp teeth sank into her flesh.

"NO!!! Help me please! Arrrggggg!"

Kimberlane lurched up, clutching the front of her gown wildly and looking from side to side then straight into the cold, cold darkness. A jangling at her door drew her attention. And then he was there in her room—the blinding light shown in her face.

"What's wrong?" A frantic voice rang out, "What's going on in here?!"

"Father! I thought you'd never come." Strong arms gripped her shoulders and shook her gently. "Daddy, you're here." She heard herself say as she threw her head into his chest and held on for dear life.

He held her and held her and held her some more. A feeling she had never experienced before engulfed her. She didn't have a name for this new sensation but safe was close. Before she could get used to it, the hands that had held and comforted her were holding her face close to his. He was speaking softly but clearly, "Are you all right, Miss Steel? Miss Steel, can you hear me?"

She shook herself. What in the world was going on? "Mr. Johnson, please take your hands off me."

"What?"

"I said, please let me go."

"Okay." With that he released her.

"Why are you still sitting here?"

James stared into her eyes. "The reason is obvious to me. What I don't understand is why it's not obvious to you."

Kimberlane ever so slowly realized that she had a death grip on James. Her words had said one thing but her body quite another. She was holding his arms so tightly, she was sure he must be bruised. She released him.

He jumped to his feet and turned his back, "You're okay then?"

Kimberlane caught sight of her appearance in the mirror: her sheer nightgown, disheveled hair, and tousled covers. She felt humiliated.

"You can leave now."

"Is that your way of saying, 'thank you'?" James smiled over his shoulder.

"Thank you?" She snorted. "Thank you for breaking into my apartment and getting involved in things you have no business?"

"No...thank you for waking me from the most horrendous nightmare I've ever had." James turned careful not to look directly at her, "And thank you for sparing me further discomfort tonight. How about that, for starters!" His hands flew as he spoke.

Kimberlane couldn't make herself answer. So James turned and left. Would the guilt of that evening never leave her? She was sorry, so sorry. She'd never be able to atone for her wrong. Wasn't that enough? She had tried to make it better by helping children. Why hadn't her grandfather stopped Eleanor, stopped her? She needed him and he didn't do a thing; he was weak and apparently so was she. Phantom father, absent grandfather; there wasn't a man in the world that could stand to be around her. But...James, his arms had swallowed her, every part: strong and unwavering. Could a man like him keep her safe? Could a man like him protect her?

James stormed back to his apartment. He slammed the door so hard that the lamps on both sides rattled.

"Ridiculous woman!" He shouted into the darkness. Her being white was only one of her problems. The woman was a bona fide schizophrenic: one moment kind, the next moment poison, one day confident, the next day a mess. She was the last woman in the world he needed occupying his thoughts and disturbing his orderly existence. Holding on to him like her life depended on it at the same time telling him to let her go like he was some kind of masher. What in the world was wrong with her? *Lord, will I ever understand women?*

"Not without my help." James' head snapped to attention. He could have sworn he had just heard— no…his imagination was getting the best of him.

The light of day shown through the balcony windows as Kimberlane traipsed through her living room still wearing the silk gown that he had touched. She pulled it tightly about her and lifted the lace to her face, could she still smell…what had she done? Make a complete fool of herself, that's what, and there was nothing for it but to make it right. She pulled her robe from the closet, the thick quilted one, wrapped it about her shoulders and made the long trudge down the royal-blue carpeted hall, looking one way then the other at the silver numbers on the door; which one would say James Johnson to her? She had walked the entire length of hall before she remembered that he'd said that he lived only a short way from her so she headed back again. Click-click, one lock then another tumbled and he was out and walking fast in the opposite direction. He really was going to make her work for this. "James, er...Mr. Johnson, do you have a minute?"

"Miss Steel, how nice to see you!" He had his back turned to her and his greeting dripped of sarcasm but she wouldn't be deterred.

"Mr. Johnson, or should I call you James; after all, you have been in my bedroom."

That got his attention. He turned. "Miss Steel, if you didn't scream out like a banshee being hounded by the devil himself—"

"Self-saboteur," she mumbled.

"What's that?" James demanded.

"I said, Mr. Johnson." He looked very nice in his crisp pleated pants, "and can I please call you James; I said that I have a habit of sabotaging myself. Here I am trying to apologize for how badly I treated you last night and I keep putting my foot in my mouth. May I start over?"

"You may," he said, crossing his arms and smiling, "I think this is gonna be good."

"James," she looked to him for his approval which a subtle nod admitted, "I'm very sorry for how I treated you last night. I know that at times I yell like a...what was that you said...oh yes, a banshee. I have nightmares or howling-mares as my aunt deemed them, owed in no small part to the experiences I endured daily under her auspices..."

"I'm sorry, Miss Steel, but you're rambling."

"Sorry, again. I'm no good at this; can you come over and have dinner with me tonight? Maybe I can demonstrate my contrition better than I can say it."

"Maybe you can," he said as he marched off with a curl of his lip that Kimberlane thought was somewhere between disgust and extreme satisfaction. "I eat at six."

"What an arrogant—"

"What's that, Kimberlane?" By now she was at her door, which she gave an unceremonious slam in his wake.

8

❦

Making Up Is Hard To Do

SIX P.M. SHARP. JAMES KNOCKED LIGHTLY.
Why not give her a chance; she was trying. He put his
ear to the door: nothing. He knocked harder: still
nothing. She had to be there—didn't he tell her he ate
at six; wasn't she trying to apologize? He stood
shaking his head. She wasn't even home. Good joke.
As he turned he heard rustling: paper bags, bottles
clinking and tin cans clanging.

"Kimberlane, Kimberlane Steel? It couldn't be.
Are you the woman who's making me an apology
dinner?"

"James, forgive me. I had a job interview and
well…can you help me with these bags?"

James frowned since he was already taking the
bags from her hands as she spoke.

"I went to that center, the one Mike told me
about; your godson Charlie plays there sometimes.
Well, they said I could start next week. I really like
being around children and it helps me—"

"Helps you?"

"I mean, it's just that I really love kids."

"Me, too. If I were…"

77

"If you were what?"

"Nothing. How was Charlie?"

"He didn't say much. Kinda stayed to himself. But he gave me a big hug."

"It's odd how he likes you."

"You think it's odd that someone would like me?"

"No, Miss Steel, despite our many, I don't know…skirmishes, I think deep inside you are a good person. Maybe just a little unsure." James took the key from her hands.

"And I think, Mr. Johnson, that we should decide once and for all to call each other by our first names and to get this dinner started."

"Okay, Miss, er…Kimberlane, what have you got?" The door was unlocked.

"I've got steak, chicken, pork chops—"

"Vegetables?"

"Oh my goodness…"

"You did remember vegetables and maybe bread?"

"I was so intent on making sure I had something you liked and I haven't cooked in a very long time."

James chuckled to himself.

"I know what you're thinking…you're thinking I obviously know how to cook or I wouldn't be this way." Kimberlane stalked over to the refrigerator and starting tossing meat in as the frosty waves escaped.

James was trying hard to understand what had happened. "Well, I know you have some cans and bottles; I heard them clanging."

"I have pop and peaches. I was going to make you a pie. Now you can just leave."

"Have I done something to upset you?"

"You just insinuated that a person of my size couldn't have gotten this way without cooking, and if you are going to be mean—"

"Hold on just one minute. I never said or insinuated any such thing."

"You did, too," she snapped, slamming cans on the counter, "I saw you chuckle when I said I didn't cook much."

"Kimberlane, are we still in first-name territory? I chuckled thinking of someone going through so much trouble to please me, that's all; I think it's nice and I think you're nice. Is that okay?"

Kimberlane watched his mouth as she had done so many times before. The shapeliness of his lips and the fine sculpt of his mustache mesmerized her as he tried to disguise his command of the language—despite herself she sat. It seemed somewhere he had gotten the message that a Negro man ought not to speak so properly. She found herself with her arms propped on the Lucite kitchen table, gaping at his mouth, not caring at all what he was saying, just wanting to watch him talk. He was up—where was he going?

"What are you doing?" she said, getting to her feet.

"Going to my place—I've got some canned corn and some squash in the fridge. You like yellow squash?"

"Sure, what do you want for meat?"

"Surprise me."

James returned to find Kimberlane sawing back and forth with an excruciatingly dull knife on a chicken which would have been handled much better with a few hacks of a butcher's blade which he had in his kitchen. He figured to get it would embarrass her further so he let her continue to try.

He found her can opener and worked it around the top of a tin of corn. Then he sliced the yellow squash and heated some oleo in a skillet. "Need some help with that chicken?"

"No, I've got it," she said with her back to him.

He could see she didn't have it. He walked to where she stood and peered over her shoulder. "Let me help." He reached for the knife and she caught his hand shoving it into the chicken, which landed on the linoleum floor with a clack rather than a thud. "Is that bird frozen?" James howled before he could catch himself. Then with no mercy for her feelings at all he doubled over laughing.

"You stop that, James Johnson, this isn't funny."

Did she have tears in her eyes? He tried to straighten up and come to her rescue. "I'm sorry," he began.

"You ought to be," she said, reaching for the chicken and bumping heads with James who was also reaching for it. "Ouch!" she yelled with so ludicrous a squeal that she started laughing, too. "Now you've done it. You've really cooked our goose."

"What," James said lifting the semi-frozen bird by its plastered-down arms, "Why, madam!" He pantomimed with the icy bird while shaking with laughter, "I most certainly am not a goose and I shan't be cooked in a million years no matter how hard you try."

Kimberlane laughed despite herself. It was funny; she was no cook. Whatever skills she possessed were long lost. Luxury and lack of necessity had drained away any cooking ability she might have possessed under other circumstances. "I can't cook, James."

"No...you must be joking." He was still laughing at her but it didn't seem mean. He was looking at her as if he wanted her to join him, so she did. She laughed so that her side ached and it felt good.

"Come here," he said lifting her to her feet, "let's just sit and talk for a while to get to know each other. I can eat anytime. It's not often that I get to chill out and really get to know someone."

Kimberlane followed him to the second-hand couch Mike brought over the day she moved in. It was a little tattered but she had covered it with one of the blankets she took from the hotel. It was a luxuriant deep red that completely covered the shabbiness of the couch. She had left more than enough money on her hotel bed to cover its cost. She could have sat in one of the kitchen chairs that came with the apartment. She had placed two of the four in the living room but for some reason she chose to sit on the couch not too near but not too far from James.

"James, why haven't you ever married?" What was wrong with her? Had she really bumped her head this hard?

"Never found the right girl, I guess."

He didn't seem to notice the intimacy of the question. Good. "What about Shelly Madison?" *Lord, help me*.

"What do you know about her?"

Think, Kimberlane, think. "Er...everyone knows about..."

"Ahh, about my infamous misstep," James cut in. "I didn't know you and Mike had become such fast friends. I assume he told you about us."

Kimberlane breathed a big sigh; that last question could have been her undoing. "Oh yes, I was just thinking: she's such a good girl and all."

"You talk as if you know her." James narrowed his eyes as if trying to figure her game.

"I just wonder why a nice guy and a supposedly nice woman wouldn't get together, that's all."

"She was in love with another man, that's all—simple."

"And you really loved her?" she asked, inching very close to his smooth lips and allowing her neck to crane so she could take in the rich amber in his eyes.

"I thought I did." Now he was looking deeply into her eyes. Sweat eased down her blouse and she felt lightheaded. His piercing gaze bore into her. "I don't feel so good," she heard herself say.

"Lay your head…"

Now she was embarrassed; he was probably going to say, back, lay your head back, but before he finished his sentence, she had laid her head on his shoulder instead and it felt good.

"Kimberlane?"

"James, can you keep talking? I love the sound of your voice." The words were out before she could censor them and she wasn't sorry. She had waited for this a long time and so what if everything wasn't in its proper order. When had her life ever followed an orderly flow? And besides, his voice was like rushing waters, forceful and calming. She felt the rhythm inside her grow steady.

"Kimberlane." He wanted to know she was still listening. She was sort of. She heard something about Shelly, which she mostly ignored. Apparently she had passed on James. Any woman who could look at this six-foot-two, hewn-muscled, dark shimmering warrior and say 'no' was not worthy of her attention. He briefly touched on his mother and father, both dead, and his deadbeat brother, who might as well be dead. But when he got to Charlie, her ears perked.

"How long have you known him?"

"Not long at all." James removed his arm and sat forward. He ran his left hand over his chin, "That's the funny thing, months really."

"Where are his parents?"

"No one knows. Mrs. Timmons got him from a friend of hers who took care of him for a few days when his foster mother died suddenly. By all rights she should have turned him over to the state. Said it was okay since she was licensed to foster. I don't think she wanted to see him go back into the system right away. Poor kid, he's been passed around and around."

"Sounds like me," she whispered off to the side.

"Now Mrs. Timmons says she can't keep him. It's a shame." He turned to face her. "He's a good kid. Called me godfather or Mr. James from the first day I met 'em. Can't make up his mind, I guess. Probably waiting for me to make up mine."

Kimberlane put her hand on top of his. He smiled.

"How'd you two meet?"

"Humph." He laughed. "It was December. So cold only a bunch of foolish kids and a woman determined to keep a promise would be out. I was takin' the shortcut through the park when I saw Mrs. Timmons holding her collar with one hand and two kids with the other. She was shakin' like a leaf."

"She asked you to take 'em."

"You got it."

"Dependable James." She smiled.

"That's me. Snow was fallin' like meatballs. I was about to tell her it wasn't gonna happen. That the best thing she could do was get all those children home before everybody got pneumonia. Then he piped up 'Please, Mr. James.' I looked down to find this strange-looking boy peeping from behind her skirt. He was a little too light, big eyes and a funny smile. 'All of the children want to.' He grins. I took to him right away. Reminded me of my brother Jasper when he was cute and concerned about other people."

Kimberlane could see sweetness and sorrow in James' soulful eyes.

"'They'll be mad at Mrs. Timmons if we don't go.' That Charlie wasn't about to take 'no' for an answer. I asked him his name. Charlie Drake. Liked him right away. Kinda mushy, huh?"

"No, I think it's lovely." She went quiet.

"What you thinking?"

"Lots of things...I used to know some Drakes. That's not a very common name."

"No, guess not."

"But it must be common enough," she laughed.

"Obviously." He relaxed and put his arm back around her shoulder like it was the natural thing to do. "Anyway..." She could feel his taut muscles and she wondered what it'd feel like to be wrapped in his powerful grip. To be unable or unwilling to move because he had her. "...we've been unofficial family since. He's a good boy, thoughtful and real. For some reason I want to protect him. To see him grow up. I think that's why I feel so badly about not taking him myself. I just don't—"

Kimberlane placed her finger over his moving lips. "I believe you'll know what to do when the time comes. Try not to worry about it so much."

Kimberlane could feel Charlie's pain, she could feel her own, she could feel James' and she wanted to do something to stop it. She looked up at James' mouth again and for the second time this evening did something she'd wanted to do for a very long time. She snuggled closer, closed her eyes and tugged on his chin. For two seconds she thought he wouldn't— then he did. This kiss sent all her senses to flash. She had never experienced anything like it. She wanted to scream. Instead she jumped to her feet. Her nerves were jangled. She didn't know how to do this.

"Do you like this dress? I just picked it up. You don't think it makes me look fat?"

He was tearing at the newspaper, which sat on her lamp table. "Kimberlane, what size do you wear?"

"Nine." *Ten, twelve, seven…*

"Only a nine?" He seemed distracted. Working the newspaper anxiously. Suddenly his eyes were back on her. "I think it's pretty. I think you're pretty."

She refused to meet his gaze. Instead she peered at her figure in the balcony glass.

"So you think I'm pretty, really?" She looked back for confirmation.

"Kimberlane," he stepped up behind her, melding their reflections in her balcony window, "I don't know who tried to mess you up but there is no doubt that you are pretty, and you are not fat." He was pulsing in her ear and she felt herself melting. "I think you're beautiful." From behind his back he produced a perfect newspaper flower.

"When did you do that?"

He put his arms around her. "When you were standin' there scrutinizing yourself." He placed the stem in her hand.

"I was…" She tried to turn but he was behind her, too close. She could feel his body pressing hers. It wasn't right, but then again it was so right. Then he did something strange. He placed his hand on her stomach and pressed in. Her body froze. Her belly, the source of such painful emptiness…his hands were there and instead of feeling empty she felt full, fulfilled. Suddenly she imagined her legs entwined around his body. She became lightheaded, everything inside her wanting. She could no longer stand on her own two feet. "James," she heard herself moan. He lifted her. She could feel him; them, tilting toward her bedroom. *No,* her thoughts echoed but her voice refused to utter. She couldn't even hear herself.

She didn't want this. To be taken again. Her fiancé had been her only lover and only pain had come from that. She couldn't let this happen. Not again.

James looked up to find himself and Kimberlane surrounded by a sumptuous four-poster bed. Were they in the same apartment? This bed was the most luxurious thing he'd ever seen, even more extravagant than that golden couch she had in the front room still sitting on packing blocks. The mattress, like a floating cloud beneath them, was taking them over.

He felt the heat of her breath on his neck, then his chest. His arms had wound their way so tightly around her waist that he felt he'd squeeze the life out of her. He wanted to stop to think of a reason he shouldn't, he couldn't; but her hands were everywhere and so were his. He wound his fingers into her hair and held her face between his hands; the passion and the familiarity he saw there frightened him.

Kimberlane lay beneath James, gazing into his sultry eyes. She stroked the raven hair above his ear and inhaled deeply the scent of him. Suddenly shy, she closed her eyes and felt his lips heavy on hers, moist, insistent. She was being swallowed, eaten alive and she loved every luscious moment of it...but—"James, do you...I mean aren't you hungry?" James continued his onslaught. She asked her question again, "James, don't you want to go get some..."

That did it. The spell was broken.

He sprung from the bed. "Now that you mention it, how 'bout some Franco's?" he said, pushing his shirt into the waist of his pants.

"Okay, but that's blocks away. It'll take a while, won't it?"

She scooted to the edge of the bed, just now getting her breathing under control.

"Yeah, well good sauce can't be rushed."

"No, no, it can't. We want it to be right," she gasped. "Take your time."

"Sure," James was saying as he reached for his button-down sweater. "Okay, see you when I get back." He pressed a sincere kiss on her forehead.

James had totally blanked out the blocks it took to get to Franco's and the looks he must have gotten as he staggered through the dark air staring down at the cement sidewalk. One lady had actually stopped to look him up and down. That's when he noticed that his gray sweater had been half tucked into his pants, while his shirt was half pulled out. Something felt tight at his ankle. Ahh his left sock was pulled over the top of his pant leg. It's a wonder he had not been arrested. And now he was peering down at meal choices for tonight.

James tried to collect his thoughts: Like Dorothy's tornado, he had whipped her up into a ferocious storm. Hovering over that enormous bed of hers, they were kissing. Her mouth was so sweet, he had to push back to make sure he wasn't dreaming and that her mouth wasn't really the most delicious candy he'd ever tasted. Just when he thought he couldn't take it anymore, neither could she. Only the result was not what he'd imagined. She pulled her sweet mouth, swollen with his kisses, away from him and said the most ridiculous thing.

"Are you hungry?" She said, "Are you hungry?" When his fuzzy brain put the words together, he said 'yes.' He actually said 'yes.' His steps were slow and decided as he made his way across the deep purple carpet toward the door. When his hand grasped the faceted glass doorknob, he gave Kimberlane one last look over his shoulder. She piped up about McDonald's, then agreed they were better off with something cooked slow. What in the world had just happened?

Kimberlane watched as James walked from her red-hot bedroom, previously beige. He kind of pin-balled off the wall outside her bedroom, then bounded to stagger toward the apartment entry. She pulled herself from her bed and swayed toward him, watching. She had never seen him helpless and she was sure he'd never been. What had she done to him? "What do you want again?" he turned to say before heading out the door. "McDonald's?" she'd blurted. He said more about a slow meal. She, barely able to stand or catch her breath, agreed. Feeling this awkward was unusual even for her.

When the door made its final click, tears leapt to her eyes. She raised her trembling hands to push away the swamp. Then she pulled her blouse back over her shoulders attempting to fasten buttons, which were no longer there. She saw the shiny blue objects next to her bed as she re-entered her room. Pausing at her clunky chest of drawers and peering into the smoky glass mirror above it, she studied her face. Her cream colored complexion was flushed with sweet pink bruising. The kisses. Her blouse was pulled and tugged to an uneven and gapping 'V', her slip scantly covering her brassiere, revealing the swell of her bosom. What was she doing here?

She looked at the light in her ebony eyes; they were again sparking with the flame of love's hope. Did James love her? Kimberlane smoothed the threatening curly strands of her hair that had fallen from its pins back into place. She didn't like when her hair came undone, even in unguarded moments.

What she felt for James was certainly real but hadn't she felt exactly the same way on the eve of her marriage to Ashton?

I can't be here. Kimberlane ripped her pale blouse away and rummaged through her top drawer for the first thing she could find. With hands still trembling, she shook out a peach cotton shirt and wrapped it around her shoulders. Quickly she fastened the buttons she could while ignoring the rest. She hoisted up her sagging black skirt, tugging on the metal side zipper and pushed her feet into the first pair of pumps in her closet. Hangers clanged as she yanked out a thin shawl for the night air. Snatching up her purse, she fled her apartment like a thief. She wasn't about to do this again. Passion wasn't love.

For a man who was about to be thoroughly satisfied, James moved meticulously slow. He had been in a few sex-only relationships, two to be exact. One had happened when he was only sixteen. Mrs. Willow had decided he looked old for his age and needed a little worldly experience. She invited him to her house when her husband wasn't home and taught him a few things. That whet his appetite and he initiated the second encounter on his own after leaving high school. When he found out he really wanted Shelly, he was determined to wait for her. What a waste. He liked Kimberlane and if she was willing, he was going to have her, tonight.

So, why was he standing—head bowed, arms stretched out on the glass counter of Franco's—rumpled, bleary-eyed, confused and puzzling over just the right thing to get her for dinner. The thick round pasta looked good. Did she like tomato sauce? What about that zucchini with those tiny onions or would she rather have an iceberg salad? There was some kind of fancy meat. Was it veal, maybe lamb? Which would Kimberlane prefer? God, why did he care? Blam! The glass rumbled. The counter girl fled.

James looked toward the big Italian in a dark suit who was glaring at him. He had been eating quickly and talking with his hands. His neck-tucked pale napkin bleeding red from the constant flow of pasta sauce he wiped from his chin. Now he and the thin blonde with the slim legs were looking at him. He, rather than her legs, was now the object of everyone's whispered comments.

"Hey...what do you think! James, James Johnson, is that you?" The heavily accented deep-throated voice sounded.

"Yes, Mr. Franco," he ground out, "it's me."

"Something wrong, son? You don't look too good."

"My apologies, Mr. Franco." James waved the restaurant owner off, "I'm okay. Don't worry."

"Sure, James, sure. No more pounding on the counter, capisce?"

"Yeah, sure, not a problem."

This was maddening, not figuring out what she wanted but figuring her out. Why in the world did she matter to him? And so soon.

What was he doing here? The glare light of the restaurant was a stark contrast to the dark of the night. James looked down at his wrinkled pants and shook his leg. He hadn't planned on being out tonight. Just like he hadn't planned on putting in a good word for Kimberlane when they asked him about her at the center. "She really loves children," JoAnne, the center's secretary had said. "Your tenant keeps coming in to check and see when we can interview her. She even played with the kids in her suit and heels while she waited for us to talk with her." That was the thing that James admired most about her. She clearly had money and breeding yet she was concerned about people who did not. She could spend her time in high society but she chose rather to spend it in peewee society. That made him smile.

As James thought about what he had planned on doing, seducing the very welcoming Miss Steel, he decided he hadn't planned any of this. Unacceptable. If Miss Steel didn't have enough dignity and self-respect to stop this, he'd have to be the one to do it. James thought about how incredibly loose these 1960s women were living and he wanted no part of it. Problem was, he could still feel the downy softness of her delicate hair on his palm. He raised it to his cheek and was ashamed when he found his hand resting on his lips and his nostrils straining to recall her. "What!" He snapped as the counter lady asked him what he wanted.

It had been two days since the 'Kimberlane episode' and James had had a relapse of sorts. Inaction can cause that. Shelly and Mark again. They were back. Bloody black clouds thundered outrage as he sat behind the window contemplating the action he was about to take. He smiled thinking about it, yes, smiled. He had rehearsed it in his mind's eye a thousand times. The Sundays when Mark Schultz wasn't away on one of his famed business trips or 'they' weren't attending the church near their apartment, they would grace Mt. Prospect with their presence. They'd park his little red sports car in the overflow lot across from the church. He'd somehow manage to pull his mammoth ex-football legs from behind the steering wheel and practically leap over the hood getting to his pretty brown Shelly.

She'd look up and smile that wonderful smile. He waited for it, basked in it. He didn't move until she did. Anyway, she'd flash it, that full-toothed grin of hers. Then he'd open the door and take her hand. She'd let him. She always let him. She'd get out of the car and grab his arm. And they'd break into a cantor. That thing they did, like horses on parade.

Clutch, press, engine…don't gun it. James tells himself: smooth now, slow glide, don't accelerate. His big truck, used for hauling his moves, creeps up on the unsuspecting Romeo and Juliet. Their heads snap to attention. *They can see me now,* he thinks, *but it doesn't matter; I'm a friend.* Closer, closer…one tire rotation, maybe two, and 'deer in the headlights'. Eyes wide, no escape: blam, splat!

"Oh my god! I'm so sorry!" He's kneeling looking at their mangled bodies.

"James."

"I'm so, so sorry." The confusion is etched permanently on their faces as they stare blankly, coldly into space.

"James."

He lifts Mark's limp hand and watches it drop, "My God!"

"James, man…"

Pouncing on Shelly, he tries to revive her. To bring life back into her lungs.

"Okay, you're scaring…"

And that's the reason he'd never kill anyone. He'd have to kill his conscience first.

"James!" Someone was shaking his shoulder, violently. "James, man, what's wrong? How long you been here? You look terrible." Mike was standing over his table, yelling. The same table the big Italian and fooffie blonde had sat at Thursday night. Pangs of guilt hit him as he caught Mike's worried expression bouncing off Franco's floor to ceiling café window.

"I'm okay. Sit down." He pointed at an empty chair.

"Your pasta's like glue," Mike snapped. He'd never let food sit so long. He picked up James' drink and took a sip, "and your coffee's cold, man." He swallowed despite his pouched lips. He was clearly looking for somewhere to spit.

"Yes, it's best that way," James snorted, still eyeing Mike as a reflection in the window.

"Best cold? Okay, what are you smirking about?" Mike was shoving up the sleeves of his half-pressed dress shirt.

"Smirking?" James clasped his hands and cracked his knuckles.

"Yeah, man, what's on your mind?" Hiking his pant legs, Mike squeezed into the spindly seat at James' small Formica table and gazed at the side of is his friend's face.

"Church, just another Sunday at church." Suddenly James jerked away from the window and looked directly at his friend, "You going tomorrow?

9

Sacred Space

HE HADN'T GONE BACK to Kimberlane's place. He didn't want another sordid affair and he wasn't ready for commitment. Instead after leaving Franco's, he had wandered the night streets, head down, tearing his fingernails while peeling the sticky plastic wrap off of wine candies. He popped two of the apple and one grape Jolly Rancher in his mouth at the same time. He could swear he heard his teeth cracking as he crunched rather than sucked the small barrels. It was this distraction that caused his left shoe heel to catch on a curve, toppling him into a Pontiac stopped for the light. His ears still rang from the cursing he got from the woman behind the wheel. Fate must have been in a charitable mood, seeing the next thing he did was pick a fight with Big Eddie, one of the nicest and most gentle giants he knew.

"Hey James, you okay? You don't look so good."

"Who asked you, you pea-brained half-wit?"

"Ah, James, you must be bad off to talk like that."

"That what your father told you to say when

someone insults you, big guy?"

"Let me look at you. I don't think you are so good."

"I don't think…" he was in the process of mimicking when he noticed the light going out of Big Eddie's eyes. A very bad sign.

"Hold on a minute there, big guy." Mike appeared, wrapping Eddie in a friendly bear-to-bear hug. He was just in time to save James' bacon from the fire. No one had ever walked away from a Big Eddie brawl. It took a lot to get him going but a heck of a lot more to get him stopped. James once saw five men attempt to restrain him. Each limped away for his trouble. He'd find Eddie and apologize after church.

It was all her fault. God, Kimberlane confused him, disturbed him. He had always been a man who knew exactly what he wanted and exactly where he was going. How had this happened to him; how had any of this happened to him?

Finally. Mt. Prospect. James felt a huge whoosh exit his chest. It was a warm day. He didn't wear a suit. His short-sleeved cotton shirt caught the breeze in waves. He felt better. The towering brown brick of his church with its traditional pointed roof, looming rugged crosses both inside and out, and the arched doorway entrances gave him a feeling of comfort. His mother and father had been founding members. And his uncle Robert donated a boatload of cash over the years, anonymously of course. 'Policy running' was frowned on by many. It was here that he felt community, especially in the old days before 'they' arrived. But he was determined to keep his bastion of peace, his place of refuge. The Schultzes and nobody else could ruin it for him.

Mt. Prospect's massive doors lay open; while ladies wobbled in on their rickety heels, tan pumps, black slingbacks with matching handbags, some holding the arms of men who wore suits no matter what the weather. Children rushed, threatening to topple the gray and feeble, who laughed at, rather than yelled at, the playful kids. Church was crowded today. You could hardly see the burgundy carpet beneath the feet of the faithful.

What...no...was no place sacred? James wended his way between the gaggles of church folk, barely able to contain himself as he lurched toward his faithful friend. "What's she doing here?" He pointed toward Kimberlane who he'd just seen get up from sitting next to Mike. "Is she coming back?" he hissed at Mike who was sitting at the end of the pew, his jacket holding the place next to him.

"She, as you put it," Mike sneered at him like he had froth foaming from his mouth, "went to the lady's room. What's wrong with you, man?"

"I just don't understand why she's here." James snarled nose to nose with his friend.

Mike blew an exasperated breath, "If you really need to know, I ran into her Thursday night and she said—"

"Thursday night, where?"

"Outside your building and her current home. Is that okay with you?"

"Yeah sure, what time?"

"Uhh, let me see…I didn't exactly check my watch but I'd say two hours before I stopped Big Eddie from knocking your head off," Mike quipped, cocking a brow at James. "Anyway, she said she was a little shook up, said she was getting off track. Said she had narrowly escaped making a huge mistake."

"Off track," James stood straight. "Mistake?" he whispered into the air.

"Don't take it personally, James." Mike jokingly tried to pat his hand. "I'm sure it has nothing to do with you. Anyway, she said she was a little off track and needed to find her way."

"And you brought her here?" James leaned in again for privacy.

"Well, yes—" Mike leaned back, squinting more seriously at his face.

"Michael's a good boy and takes Our Lord's work seriously." A familiar richly brown hand fell on Mike's shoulder.

"Miss Rose." The last person he wanted to see. "I didn't notice you back there."

"That's obvious," Rose said, leaning back and clasping her strong hands over her lap. "It's equally obvious that someone's got your nose wide open." Her clear eyes were bold and knowing.

"Huh?" Mike's broad lips made a perfect "O" as he peered back at Mama Rose.

James knew exactly what Rose was saying. Mildred Atwater leaned forward so she could know better, too. James felt the neck of his collar go damp. He stumped away from the deteriorating scene. He wanted to shake it off, all of it. Why the…had he called her Miss Rose, rather than Mama Rose? He'd be paying for that. It would confirm that he was rattled. Just a matter of time before Rose came flying around for one of her 'talks'.

No sooner had he stepped into the aisle that he noticed her mincing toward him, head bowed, fumbling with the clasp of her purse. Her hair was rolled into one of those tight French things that woman did. Wispy brown curls floated around her face. A lacy collar hugged her neck and her mauve suit fit her every curve. He couldn't get out of the aisle; he'd have to speak to her; she beat him to it. "James," she looked up from snapping the silver clasp on her delicate patent leather handbag. Her eyes were puffy. All of the steam evaporated from his sail.

"I just couldn't...I'm sorry I didn't wait—"

"You didn't, did you?"

"No, it wasn't...hold on..." She stopped sniffing. Her red nose made her look like Rudolf: vulnerable and cute. "You didn't come back, did you!?"

The room froze: adults stopped chattering, babies ceased whining, pages stopped flapping, even the organist's pings jolted to a halt.

"Come with me," James shushed, grabbing her arm and leading her toward the churches arched door. "People are listening," he rasped through gritted teeth. "God, is there no place sacred?" James mumbled as they walked quickly and quietly into the bright sunlight. "First the Schultzes, now you." *Can't a man even worship without being bothered by undesirables?*

❧

"James!"

He felt his back stiffen. Not Rose. Not now. "Mama Rose—" He turned into the rushing wind and sunshine.

"Mama, huh?" Her lip twitched and the wide flopping brim of her hat waved violently. "Had time to gather your wits, have you?" She squinted against the brightness.

"Yes, ma'am, and if you don't mind I was just about to talk with Miss Steel here."

"Miss Steel, where?" She looked around him.

James snapped his head this way, then that, to see Kimberlane across the street rushing toward some neighboring trees. This realization caused him a heavy sigh.

"Mama Rose, I'm kind of busy and if you've come out here to give me the benefit of one of your talks, well I'm just not in the—"

"Hold on there, Jimmy-James, contrary to your beliefs, the sun does not rise and shine on your brown behind."

"What?"

"But since you brought it up, I can see that you are in pain."

"Pain, Mama Rose—you are way off base. If anything I'm angry, mad." His voice rose and he stepped   forward.

"About what?" She placed her hands on her hips, her suitcase of a purse threatening to tip her over.

"Well, it's not complicated. I'm tired of people intruding on my solitude."

"Is that supposed to scare me off?" Rose questioned, frowning up into his face and the blazing heat.

"I wasn't…uh…I didn't mean you exact—"

"Yes, you did; but you didn't mean me exclusively. It's thisa way, James-boy, this is precisely your problem. Everything and everyone is an intrusion to you. Each and every one who don't do exactly what you think they should. You make plans and like pawns on a chessboard you expect us to line up and get with the program. And if your relationship with my grand—"

"I don't want to talk about that," James ground out between gritted teeth.

"I know you don't, but it's time you did." She gripped his arm, "James, don't walk away from me, boy."

"Miss Rose." He turned. She wasn't there.

"Sit down here, son, right next to me," she said tugging on his pant leg. She had flopped down on the curb in her long white dress, a feat for a thirty-year-old, let alone someone who was seventy-something. "Yelling is not going to get you a pass," she yelled up at him.

James knew he couldn't avoid this, so he hoisted up his pant legs, and squatted on the hot sidewalk near her. The spry woman squished up to his side. "Now, James-Honey," she took his hand and patted it. He hated that. "It's like this, if you gone be God

Almighty," she pointed to the sky, "there's no room for Him…"

He heard an enormous groan rush from his throat. She continued to stoke his hand and despite his best efforts he was starting to feel calm—a dangerous position in Rose's presence.

"James, you're a good man but that's your problem. You see your own good and you think there's nothing to be fixed. The Bible says there's no one good, no not one." He tried to pull his hand away—he was anticipated; Rose tightened her grip. "Jesus said, God is good, no one else. So, James, don't be so proud. Bow your knee, son."

"I pray," he protested.

"James, I'm talking symbolic and I think you know that. Bend your knees, humble yourself, admit you're not in control. Ask God what He wants for you."

"And I should expect Him to answer?"

"Boy!" She gawked at him like she was seeing him for the first time, "Y-o-u a-i-n't n-o more saved than a street-house rat. Are you?" That statement pulled then snapped.

"Miss Rose!" He did snatch his hand away this time as he jumped to his feet.

"I'm sorry, James, but you ain't never known me to lie, especially about the Lord's business."

She was infuriating—more so this time than ever before and insulting, too. She didn't even give him the respect of standing to complete her insults. Just sat there pulling the flap of her hat over her eyes prattlin'. "James, listen, this is gonna change your life if you can hear."

He wanted to stalk off; he meant to, but his feet were glued to the cement.

"You, son, are arrogant, and pride comes before a fall. God Himself can have a treasure to give you but if you think you have it all He's not gonna pry your hand open. A closed fist will lose, not receive. When the gift…"

Finally his feet obeyed his command and he made his escape. She was in the middle of talking about scales on his…whatever. Maybe he should change churches. When had Baptists believed in tongues, and prophecies and interpretation, anyway? He needed a traditional church. All this extra holy stuff was starting to get on his nerves…not saved? What was 'saved' anyway? He had gone to church all his life. His family was one of the founding families of Mt. Prospect. She was the new one, the interloper, the… He stalked into the noon breeze refusing to hear what was being whispered on the wind: You don't have Kimberlane, your parents, your brother, Charlie, God. You are a lonely, lonely man.

The sky struck a confident cord, indigo filling the space beyond James' thoughts. Commanding clouds, thick and looming blocked his vision, refusing to let him see what was clear as day. Confusion sitting on his shoulders like a naughty cat refusing to move.

James dragged into the crown jewel of his accomplishments. His court-way building. Three stories of property-owner bliss. Clean, manicured, historic and modern at the same time. He hadn't used

Mike for this deal. Mama Rose, he was loath to admit, had paved his way. He could just hear her now, "My future grandson James Johnson is a good man and if you are going to sell this property, you won't find a better man to buy it." She had believed in him and now she didn't even think God did. My, how things had changed. But this place with its luxuriant lawn, knee-high wrought-iron border gates and individual balconies, was his—his home and his refuge. And today, a day with hidden sun, which still caused his shirt to stick to his chest, it would have to be enough.

After nearly breaking his key off in the lock, he huffed into his apartment recalling his irritation. He plopped down on his striped sofa, hands flying immediately to his temples. Sweat oozed from his neck to his chest while her words rolled around in his head: "Boy, you ain't no more saved than a gutter rat," or whatever she had said. The nerve of that woman, he didn't care if she was the neighborhood 'queen-all-wise-mother'. She had gone too far this time and he had a good mind to march right over to Maple Street and tell her where to get off. No wonder that granddaughter of hers put on such airs. Having Rose as a grandmother would give anybody a warped sense of importance.

And while he was thinking about women who irritated him, why not give some thought to Kimberlane. How dare she leave her apartment like he was going to come back and force himself on her. What a rip. She was the one who was all over him, giving herself to a man she hardly knew. But would a good Christian man take advantage of a woman, even one who was warm and ready? He certainly had in the past but lately he didn't want to do that and he didn't want that between him and Kimberlane. "Who am I?" he asked himself as he pushed up from the couch and headed toward the bathroom to wash his face. "James," the water seemed to murmur. "James…James…James…" as the drops from the steel faucet hit the puddle pooled in the sink. The splash swirls vibrated, "Who am I?" James mirrored the question, "Who am I?"

At twenty-nine, he looked the same as he had when he was a boy. "Still as handsome as you ever were," Pam had said, running her hand down his chest, and he guessed it was true. In high school the girls said, "His eyes invite you to dance and the small dent in his chin makes him look like a comic book hero." He shouldn't have wrinkles, but the worry of the past years had added a hint near the corner of his mouth. Shelly said it was because his face didn't get enough smiling practice. What did he have to smile about: both his mother and father had passed away, his bother Jasper was in Europe spending his share of their family's hard-earned money, and his life continued to be one big sacrifice with no reward in sight.

A week had passed, and still no Kimberlane. She must have been carefully avoiding him because he was carefully searching her out. It was time for some answers. He was going to the center to see her.

As soon as he walked through the glass door of the converted office building, he heard her.

"James, can you help me here?" Kimberlane flicked her wrist, waving him over to a little girl who was holding her leg. "Sandra has given herself a really bad scrape." She winked with that strange sometimes-familiarity. "Show Mr. James."

The young girl lifted her left knee. "But Sandra, I thought you showed me your other knee." Sandra poked her lips out and pulled up her right knee, teetering on the previously sore leg.

"Oh yeah," she said, about to fall as she balanced herself. James patted the seat next to him and Sandra sat. He gave her thin leg a good glance and shrugged. "I don't see anything. I think you're fine."

"I am not fine!" Sandra whined, "I need a Band-Aid."

"Sure, sure," James agreed. "Let me look in my pocket. Oh no," he moaned, "not a single Band-Aid but what is this?" He pulled out a small purple barrel-shaped candy wrapped in clear plastic and twisted at the ends, a Jolly Rancher. "Look what I found."

"Is that a wine candy?" Her tiny hand grabbed for his wrist, "Can I have it, please?"

"I believe this is a special wine candy. What do you think, Miss Kimberlane? Is this a special wine candy?"

"Why yes, Mr. James, I believe it is."

"You see, little miss Sandra, this wine candy," he held up the small treasure, "is especially special."

"Special?" She squinted. "Will it make me better, Mr. James?"

"Sure will." He handed the plastic tidbit to her.

"Can you unwrap it?" She looked up at him with wide eyes.

"James," Kimberlane leaned her moist mouth to touching his ear, "she has a crush on you."

*And I have a crush on you...*his mind reeled. He tilted away from her, still steaming over the fact that she left her apartment the night of their 'almost' affair.

James twisted the plastic from the candy, stripping the tiny shreds of remaining paper from the sticky ends. "Here you are, little lady." The bright-eyed ebony girl jumped from her seat. He patted her on the back. She ran off to play with the other children.

"What's wrong?" He watched Kimberlane's pretty mouth pout and her brows tighten. He knew she was wondering at the tenderness he offered the little girl. He was so much better with children and little women than he was with the full-grown kind. Somehow he expected they would...humph, he didn't know what he expected.

"Nothing," she snapped, just mean enough for James to know she was lying. "Do you have another hard candy in your pocket? My throat's been a little itchy."

"Let me feel..." He reached for her, "You do look—"

"I don't need you to feel my forehead. But you can answer a question for me. Why is it that you are so unable to offer adults any of your tender-loving care?"

"I don't have a problem with adults."

"No, just women," Kimberlane said as Sandra's bright-red skirt flounced and waved in her wake.

"No, just you."

"What are you saying?"

"Nothing. Where did I put my jacket?"

"It's on the hook in the entry. Where else would it be? James, what do you mean it's just me? Do you have feelings for me?"

"Kimberlane, I don't know what you think you heard behind the words, but I say what I mean, and I said that I had a problem with you, not that I had feelings for you."

"Oh…"

"It's not that you're…"

"That's enough, James; I'm sorry I asked."

"Listen, Kimberlane—"

Kimberlane had heard all she cared to. She shoved James's suit jacket into his arms and went into the classroom where the program's coordinator was about to give parents the sad news about the loss of summer funding and the uncertain fate of her beloved center.

This was the way it had always turned out for her. With the adults in her life, she was too fat, too thin, too pale, not pale enough. But in this place, her place of refuge with her kids, she was fully competent. She had run the office, started keeping the books, and taken care of the children. Seemed that everyday someone was let go or quit due to their dwindling revenue. She could run this place if she really wanted to. Was this her fait accompli?

10

A Missing Of The Minds

JAMES HAD GONE INTO HIS OFFICE at Johnson Brothers Moving Co. It was a small room in the back of an old warehouse where his storage business was located. It contained a huge notched wooden desk; three metal file cabinets, one for each business endeavor; and a metal table which doubled for his secretary Shirley's desk and a meeting space. Besides her, he had two other employees, three if he counted Mike, which he never did. Mike was more of a partner, the face of the business, when needed; Eddie was the brawn, his heavy lifter, who he still had to find and apologize to if he ever expected to get anything moved ever again. And there was Mac, the new guy. He sat behind his desk fiddling, moving one stack of papers, then the other.

What he really wanted to do was help Kimberlane. She had seemed run-down lately, like she might be coming down with something. Problem was, since his godson Charlie would not be there, his excuse for being there was wearing a little thin. Poor Charlie, poor him. Mrs. Timmons had taken him to Michigan to her family, a kind of a farewell tour, before placing him with the state. His heart just kept being cut; seemed every time he got close to someone, they fell away.

He shoved the papers, nearly toppling a stack to the floor. "People are quitting left and right," Kimberlane had explained when he finally went tail-tucked back to the center. "And we'll probably be losing all our funding by the end of the season. Where will all these children go, James? I hate to see them all on their own until their parents get home from work. This place is good for them." She was so worried, pacing the whole time. "I can fix this, James. With just a little time."

He hated to think of the kids not having Kimberlane, of her not having them. He also hated to think about not seeing Charlie anymore. He really wished he could do something about that. Anyway, seeing Kimberlane helped him to feel better.

He still laughed thinking about the last time he walked her home. They ventured out of their way and went through Michael's park. Soaring oaks, gold dipping sun and crisp cool breezes made Kimberlane's dizzy dancing seem like magic. Then there was the song: "Mark's Ears Can Hear." He, Mark, walked past them looking slightly back, so she started to sing: "Mark's ears can hear, Shelly my dear, hear her here, hear her there, hear her, hear her everywhere; he won? Who lost? Not us, of course. Not us, not us, not us, of course." James wondered how she knew that would amuse him. She said she had noticed that Mark's curls covered his oversized ears and if he ever cut his hair short he'd instantly lose his feminine fan club to which she would never belong. James snickered thinking about her prancing about like a wild child whispering the song against his cheek so Mark wouldn't hear, no matter how big his ears were under those curls. "Only his barber knows for sure," she clucked. Then she said, "Doing just about anything with you is fun," before twirling out of his reach.

"Penny for your thoughts," Mike interrupted, setting a large brown bag down on his unequal stack of receipts, building permits and sundry other papers, "What's on your mind?"

James smiled, "Never mind that; what's in that bag you just dumped on my desk?"

"Collaboration soup."

"Collaboration what?"

"Here," Mike said, pulling one of several jelly-sized jars from his bag. He slowly twisted the metal top off. An intoxicating aroma sprang from the glass container.

"Wow, that smells terrific!"

Mike pulled a spoon from the bag, dipped out a scoop and handed it to James.

"You make this, man?"

"No way, I told you it's a collaboration. Mama Rose and Mrs. IRENE Schultz." Mike emphasized the 'Irene' knowing how James usually reacted to the mere mention of the other Schultz lady. "They put both their family recipes together and came up with this new chicken noodle concoction. Good, right?"

"Delicious," James mumbled, his mouth full.

"It's for Kimberlane. Said she's been fighting something off."

"Hum, that explains—"

"What'd you say?"

111

"I said, she never told me."

"And she was supposed to? I didn't know you knew each other like that…do you?"

"We do. I mean…we don't. I'm not sure what I mean. Mike, do you…er…do you like the girl?"

"I don't know. I've been thinking about it…whether or not to like her."

"Man, if you gotta think about it, the answer's 'no'."

"But didn't you just ask?"

"Never mind that; better let me take that soup," James said as he rounded his large wooden desk, grabbing the big brown bag with the remaining jars of collaboration.

Kimberlane was really getting into her job, and despite James' apparent aversion to her, he had come by two or three times a week to help out after he was done with his own work at the apartment buildings. She knew he had delegated some responsibilities at the moving business and had hired a new guy. James said he was able, just needed the opportunity to prove himself. It didn't matter to Kimberlane why he was there; she enjoyed his help and the kids really liked their Mr. James. He was a natural.

She could have used him today. Putting all the donated desks back in their proper places had taken all her strength this afternoon. She felt weak and her body ached. It was worth it though. So many of the working parents had taken advantage of her summer relief program that she thought of adding more substantive food next week. Kids could stay later if a real meal was provided. James had told her that it was the parents' responsibility to provide dinner for them. She knew he was right, but not everyone had enough money to provide good meals every day; and anyway, nobody was forcing the parents to let the kids stay, and who asked him anyway.

Everyone was gone including the kids, and James hadn't been there all week, so why was he coming up the street in this direction?

"What brings you here; it's been a while?"

"My efficient staff has learned to do without me; I didn't even have to do the books. Mac, the new guy, had it all taken care of; seems all he needed was a chance. There was nothing left to do at the office." He was telling a tiny fib. Mac couldn't add two plus two. Why hadn't he said Shirley did the books? Seems he just couldn't think straight around Kimberlane. "I came by to make sure everything was in order here."

"That was kind of you but I have it under control. Would you like some coffee? Emma brewed a pot and put out some of Miss Rose's tea cakes before she left."

James looked over her shoulder to the counter. "But there's only one left."

Kimberlane found herself snickering, the last crumbs of the cookie she had just swallowed still finding their way down her throat, "I'm guilty, James, I ate them."

"All of them?"

"Most of them, I'm a big eater."

"It doesn't show."

"I guess that's a compliment."

"Why would you doubt it?"

"I'm not used to many and I certainly haven't gotten any from your direction since…"

"I think it's admirable that you spend so much time at your job." James didn't want to think about that evening. "I mean you stay here long after what must be your required time and you seem to really love the children. Not just the white ones."

"James, can we change the subject?"

"Okay let's go back to the previous one."

"Which was?"

"Your eating."

"My eating?"

"Yes, if you eat so much, how do you keep your shape?"

"You like it? I mean you think my shape is okay?"

"Kimberlane, I know I've been an ass where you are concerned but you do remember what I told you the night we almost…"

Kimberlane sat with a thud and looked up at James as if she was seeing him again, for the first time. "So you think I'm beautiful and you're sorry."

"Yes, and I am. Can we start over? Would you like to have dinner with me tonight?"

"Pick me up at six, James; this time I'll be there."

"This time, so will I."

"Hey, what's that in the bag?" she yelled after him.

11

≈

The Best Medicine

WHAT HAD POSSESSED HER to go shopping for
a new outfit? It seemed like a good idea at the time; it
was only a short bus ride and a block to walk and she
knew just what she wanted—that little smoldering
midnight number. And it just matched her glossy new
pointed-toed pumps. Speaking of shoes, her feet were
about to burst from the ones she was wearing. The
throbbing pulse had reduced her to limping the last
block home. And her feet weren't the only things
hurting, so was her back, her head and even her
eyeballs. It was nothing; if James were here, she
would simply ask him for his arm, that's all. Aunt
Mattie had warned her about long walks in dress
shoes; sometimes she just didn't think through the

things she did. 'Hard-headed' is what Aunt Mattie would say. If she had only kept the other part of that saying in mind, the part about a soft behind, perhaps she wouldn't suffer so. Kimberlane noted the stiffness in her fingers as she rambled in her purse for her keys.

Once in the apartment she leaned on the wall and tugged at the straps of her taupe Mary-Janes. Her ankles had swollen around the bands and what should have been an easy pull of the heels took a little longer to get off her now piggy-shaped feet. If she could have leaped the distance to her bedroom door and then leaped the extra bit to her bed she would have. Better yet, wouldn't it be nice to be carried. Maybe he would…well, she could hope. With great agitation she walked on what would have been her normally soft carpet, her tingling soles pounding out every excruciating step. Squinting against the pain, she fiddled for the arm of her golden George III settee where she tossed her new dress before plopping, with a swoosh, onto her soft second-hand one. She had called home to have it shipped to her. The settee was all she asked for upon her move. You'd think the money to ship it from Pennsylvania would come directly from Eloise's paycheck; she had answered the phone informing her that Eleanor was still out of the country. "Where in the world are you anyway, miss?"

"Don't answer that," Joseph, her grandfather's personal servant, chimed in. He was on the other line. "I'll handle this, Eloise. And do remember that Miss Steel is as much Mistress of Steel Manor as Eleanor." He waited for Eloise to hang up. "Don't worry, Miss

Kimberlane, I'll get your seat sent right away and I'm taking the liberty of ordering a bed for you. You must miss your Italian circular. I'll have something comfortable delivered just for you." Good old Joseph, so often her saving grace at Steel Manor. A day or two later, men had come from Walter E. Smithe to set up a lovely four-poster like the ones in her Pennsylvanian guest rooms. Leave it to Joseph to make sure she was enjoying some of the comforts of home.

The throbbing sensations were subsiding as she sank into the cushion of Mike's loaned couch. After a minute she rolled her stockings down her legs and decided she could now retrieve her new dress from the settee and hang it up so it wouldn't wrinkle before she got to wear it for James. As she lifted it, letters she had placed on the small second-hand coffee table flittered to the floor. What was this…a letter from, from him! The navy-blue silk spilled onto the carpet as she fell back on the couch.

Her hands trembled terribly as she lifted the sterling silver letter opener Eleanor had given her on her seventeenth birthday. She said it was for opening Mattie's mail that Kimberlane later found out Eleanor had personally censored. After about a year of her living in Pennsylvania, this maneuver was no longer necessary since Mattie no longer wrote.

His letter—

My Dear Sweet Kimberlane,

It is me, your one and only Ashton. I know you have wanted to know where I've been all these years. After leaving the States and you, I moved to Paris and opened several galleries showcasing my work. I've been here doing the thing that I loved, that I thought would bury my pain. None of this—time, space, or occupation—has dulled my feelings for you.

"Feelings, what feelings?" Kimberlane mused aloud.

But your apparent betrayal was unbearable to me. I'm so sorry that my pain kept me from speaking directly to you about this instead of running off like a wounded child; but let me get to the heart of my letter. I've only just discovered the treacherous plot hatched against us. Seven years ago on the morning that we were to be married, your aunt Eleanor came to me with proof that you had been unfaithful to me.

"Proof, what proof?" Kimberlane hissed.

She produced Lyle Lancaster who I knew you to be friendly with. He convinced me that he was your true love and you had in fact been intimate with him for several months leading up to our nuptials. But this would have been nothing if she had not told me you were also pregnant.

"But I wasn't…"

At first I was furious, and then I was heartbroken. And as I said I buried myself in my work until early this month when my father asked me to cover for him in his London offices and this is where I became reacquainted with your aunt Eleanor. She confessed lying about the whole affair and she was ashamed of what she had done to me, her longtime friend.

"Ashamed of what she had done to you? What about to me, her flesh and blood? She had no reason to believe I had been intimate with Lyle."

Prepare yourself, Kimberlane, she also told me about our baby. The baby, she felt her breathing go shallow.

"James!"

Her aunt had been with her that treacherous day. She had promised by all-that-was-holy that she would never utter a word about the...

"James!"

If Kimberlane could have done anything different, she would have. For years every baby she saw was like a flaming arrow shot through her heart and later every child reminded her of every mistake she'd ever made.

"James!"

No matter how much Eleanor and Dr. Lovejoy had reassured her that it was the only thing she could have done.

"James!"

She felt there was an evil that tarnished her so deeply she'd never be able to escape it. That was until she started working at the center. It was beginning to have a healing effect.

"James, please, James, help me!" she heard herself scream at the top of her lungs.

For the second time James had run as fast as his legs would carry him to Kimberlane's apartment. These banshee yells were the most ominous he had heard. Why was she sleeping before their date? This must have been her most horrifying dream of all. He didn't believe much in psychiatrists but this woman apparently needed one badly. What had she experienced that caused her this kind of inner pain? To his dismay he didn't need to use his key to unlock her door: unlocked again. She sat staring into space, a piece of paper dangling from her trembling hand.

"James," she squealed, nearly out of voice, "help me, please."

"Kimberlane, what's wrong?"

"Help me. I need you to…I need you to read this, help me read this letter please…I can't breathe." Hiccupping, she fanned her hand in front of her face.

All James heard was that she needed him. "I'm here, Kimberlane, let me have the letter." He slipped it from her hand.

"My Dear Sweet Kimberlane," he read aloud.

"No, I read that part; from here, please." She pointed to the place she had apparently left off.

James tried desperately to read over what she had already seen but he had to get to the part she wanted before he could take it all in. "She also told me about our baby," he read. "You have a child," he heard himself say, his voice unintentionally dejected. She shrugged. He wanted to shake her but she was messed up. He continued, "Eleanor confessed lying about the whole affair to me."

"What is he saying, James? Why would Aunt Eleanor betray me, my baby is dead…I, I kil…" She leaned off the edge of the couch and melted into his arms. Those were among the last intelligible things she said for the next few days.

"I need something to drink, James. Can you get me some water, please?"

"Sure, sweet hea…" his voice trailed off as he lifted her into his arms and hefted her to the bed where she sat limply. "Kimberlane, where do you keep your glasses?" he called from her clean but disorganized kitchen. Nothing seemed to be where it should be. He had to bend to retrieve the glasses from the lowest possible cabinet; seemed she did everything differently from him.

"James."

"I'm here." When he returned to the room, she was lying fully clothed, including one stocking shoved down around her ankle, on top of her covers. "Let me," he said as she pushed at the heel of one foot with the toe of the other. He slipped the stocking off of her reddening foot.

She let out a long exasperated, "Shuuuuu." Then the tears came, big fat globs; then the trembling, then something that resembled convulsions. James lunged for her with one hand while using the other to dial. "Mama, can you come over; we need you."

Negros tended to call Mama Rose when emergency sickness set in. She was quicker than the ambulance and often knew as much as any doctor. Not to mention the prayers; James didn't like to admit it, being a rational man and all, but the prayers seemed to be the key to the whole thing. So he called her: the only person he trusted to help what ailed Kimberlane and perhaps what was now ailing him.

Upon hearing shuffling in the living room, James jumped to greet his guest. "Mama Rose, thank you so much for coming. Kimberlane needs you."

"Well, don't just stand there; get out of my way, son." Mama Rose marched into Kimberlane's room to find her on the bed writhing and whining. She had pulled the sheet into a bunch and was gnawing on it. Her legs were pulled into a knot and she rocked herself from side to side. Mama Rose sat next to her and put the back of her hand up to Kimberlane's forehead. "She's a little warm but not enough to bring this on."

"When she yelled for me, I thought she was having another one of her nightmares."

"She talks in her sleep then."

"How would I know, Mama?"

"Just checkin'." Rose's mouth twisted into a curl.

"I don't know if she talks in her sleep. But I know she yells like somebody's tryin' to kill her." He plopped down on the edge of the bed rubbing Kimberlane's back and explaining, "Not every night, fortunately, but often enough. So I was in my apartment and I could hear her calling for me." He clasped both her hands in his. "When I got here she was crying and then this started happening."

"What's this?" Mama Rose bent down to pick up the crumpled paper at the foot of the bed.

"Oh yeah, there's that. Mama Rose, I think she has a baby. Did you know she had a kid?"

"James, this girl has been a mystery to me since her arrival. I've only seen her a time or two. I don't know what she has or who she is?"

"How can she not know she had a child?" he said a little too loudly.

"James, James, snap out of it, boy. Something's set this girl into a kind of shock. Did you finish the letter?"

"No, she got sick and I called you." He scooted closer to her and noted Mama Rose's subtle squint.

"I think we should read it, James; there is more here than meets the eye. Now, where'd you leave off?"

"Here: Eleanor confessed…" James pointed to the wadded stationary.

Eleanor confessed the whole affair to me. It is astonishing. I am coming to you shortly with news you'll have to hear in person to believe. News of the child.

Forever yours, Ashton

"I can't do a thing for her," Mama Rose said, her eyes awash with something that resembled grief and pain.

"What do you mean?" James grabbed hold of her and shook. "This is what you do."

"No, not today. Today, son, it's gonna be what you do." Mama Rose reached up and firmly pulled his hands from her shoulders. "Stay here with her 'til she gets better. She called you and with the help of the Lord, well, she knows what she needs."

"You don't mean me." He whipped around, "I'm going to call an ambulance."

"You do that and when they get here the first thing they'll wanna know is why a Negro is attending a half-naked white woman. And when they're full done with you, they'll likely take her to the crazy house, first for having you here, then for whatever sickness she does or doesn't have. No, you stay here with her until she's well. It's the best medicine. You called for my advice—now you got it. Lydia Cane is having a bout of the rheumatism; I've gotta get her dinner delivered."

"It's the best medicine," James mimicked as he heard the door close behind Rose. Crazy old woman; what'd he know about nursing a crazy young one?

"James…" Kimberlane's hair had twisted out of its normal bun. It was thick and wild. She had begun thrashing and mumbling incessantly, "I did it. I'm guilty. But my child's alive, how can my baby be alive, James? Can my baby really be alive? I'm cold, James. I'm so cold. Please hold my hand, James."

James sat on the side of the bed. He stroked Kimberlane's hand and pushed her hair out of her face. Restlessly she pulled on her clothes and his. "James, help me to get out of these things. Everything feels so, so tight."

"I told Mama Rose we needed her." He looked helplessly for the ghost of Rose.

"Who…" She arched her back like a sudden pain had struck, "Please, Aunt Mattie, can you get the zipper?"

"Kimberlane, it's me, James, not Aunt Mattie."

"I know, James. James, everything feels so tight."

James reached for the phone.

"No please, please don't call him." She was rolling and writhing, "Dr. Killjoy will hurt the baby."

There's nothing wrong with her body, James. She needs a few days of love and care. Trust me, this will pass.

James thought he might hate Mama Rose at this moment but he honestly never knew her to be wrong about…well, anything, so he'd call Shirley, his secretary and let her know he'd be 'away' for a few days. She'd handle assigning duties for the moving and storage business. She'd also call Mike about the properties. And he, well, he'd call the center, then he'd be Kimberlane's nurse. He sure hoped this racked him up some points in heaven. He couldn't figure out why else he was doing it.

James had undressed her and taken her to the bathroom—thankfully she nodded 'yes' when he asked her if she could manage 'the rest' alone. The sink was positioned low and right next to the toilet. She could lean on it. "James, I'm all alone in the world," she mumbled when he came to retrieve her. "Aunt Mattie is dead. She's dead, James. No one told me. I came here and found out by accident. My grandfather...so white and Eleanor; James, she's my aunt, too. My flesh and blood. She's supposed to love me," Kimberlane rasped. She was becoming more hysterical as she rambled, "They changed me, James. They said it was because of the accident but she wanted me to look like them. I know she did. James, I'm so alone. I have no one. The baby...could the baby be... Oh James, read it again."

"My Dear Sweet Kimberlane..."

"I can't hear you, James." She was now lying back in her bed. He sat near the pillows. "Louder, please." He lifted her head and carefully placed it on his thigh, stroking the side of her face with the back of one hand as he continued to read, "...news of the child."

"News of the child," she twisted to claw his shirt, reaching to pull his face to hers. Looking wildly into his eyes she breathed the words again, "News of the child. What is he talking about, James? Why is he saying these things to me? Why now?"

Exhaustion filled James' entire being and he gave in. He didn't sleep on the tight stern royal golden settee thing, he didn't sleep on the covered worn couch and he didn't sleep on the floor. He pulled off his heavy work shoes and thick socks and balled himself into a tight knot face-to-face with Kimberlane on her luxury bed that didn't match a thing in her mismatched room. He peered into her tumultuous eyes and felt them grow calm just as he closed his own.

"Stay with me," he heard her whisper.

"I'm not going anywhere," he might have replied as he succumbed to welcome sleep.

After the third day Kimberlane began to revive. She turned in her sumptuous four-poster bed and tugged none-too-gingerly on the long pink sash that hung from the post nearest her. "Is anyone coming? Can anyone hear me?" she yelped.

"I can hear you loud and clear, which is good. You haven't been able to talk above a whisper in days. How can I help you, Empress? That piece of fabric you're yanking on isn't hooked to any intercom, you know. Seems somebody's been used to servants."

"Oh," she pulled up to her elbows, "can we talk about that another time?" Her hand flew to block the sun's coming rays. "Right now I'd love something to eat, just anything."

"I have just what you need. I thought you'd be able to eat today so I've thawed some collaboration."

"Sounds like a business deal; I'd rather have some food."

"And so you shall." He leaned to kiss her cheek. She looked surprised. He smiled.

James sauntered into Kimberlane's kitchen, grabbed a huge wooden spoon from a tall glass jar with an unusually small opening. Seemed she had her own way of doing the simplest of things. "Do you smell that?" he yelled as he stirred the thick bubbling dumpling-noodle-filled chicken concoction. It was as intoxicating as it had been the day Mike uncapped the stuff in his office. Funny, he couldn't bring himself to eat it until she could. He gave himself a silent kick while lifting the gooey spoon to his mouth for a sample. "Delicious," he moaned aloud.

"A little something for the sick woman," he sang rounding the corner to her room.

Kimberlane bolted forward.

"Hey you, not so fast. You haven't been up in days. Can you sit up?"

"Nooo," she gasped, "I'm lying back down."

"Coming." James laid the bowl alongside a tepid glass of ginger ale and quickly propped pillows behind her back.

"At least part of that looks and smells good," she smiled brilliantly. "That glass of warm pop's gonna make me sick all over again."

"Enough sarcasm. Time to get some food in you." He sat on the bed at her side and began spooning the gooey goodness into her. Her smile between chews was even bigger, then came the tears.

He froze. "What's wrong? Something hurt?"

"No, no." She tried laughing and speaking, her

mouth still full.

He realized he was holding his breath until she finally spoke.

"James, why are you so good to me?" Her pretty hand was resting on his chest. "You don't owe me anything. We're not even really close."

"Kimberlane, don't kid yourself anymore. I don't intend to. You and I both know we were about to become much better acquainted and quickly. I've finally admitted it's what I want; can you do the same?"

She could, she might as well; but she wouldn't, not right now. Couldn't a sick woman at least have a day to get on her feet before admitting that someone had just swept her off of them?

"Soup, please," was her response to James' question and implication. Tomorrow she might admit more.

James was rolling from one side to the other. This was the first night he'd slept in his small bed since the evening Kimberlane called him to her apartment to read the mystery letter. It literally made her sick, he thought, as he tried rolling to his stomach and resting on his forearms. Something so wrong had happened to her. It couldn't be her fault. It just couldn't be. He rolled to his back, his eyes plastered to the ceiling. Who, and more importantly, what was Ashton to her? Did she really have a child and not know about it? What was this foul pit of vipers she called family?

And most important of all, despite all that, was she beginning to feel for him what he now knew he felt for her?

❧

Kimberlane heard the knock but couldn't believe it. She had slept late into the morning, if it could still be called morning at eleven-thirty. She wasn't sick anymore but wished she was. If she was, James would still be in her apartment, maybe even in her bed. "Who is it?"

"Me, James."

She bounded from the bed with energy she hadn't had since she was a child.

"Be right there. What brings you here?" she announced while yanking the door open.

"You," he said, his words like sweet molasses. Her eyes closed for a minute savoring the sensation of his pronouncement. "Well, are you up to it? I know it's a lot to ask of a woman who was just two days ago on her death bed."

"Up to what?" she snapped to attention.

"The church bazaar of course. Money for the urchins and after that, the talk. I made you some breakfast a damn sight better than Woolworth's, too." It was funny; the more comfortable he became with her, the more he was like the boy she remembered: sure and smart, not pretending, not downplaying his intelligence.

"I'm not ready, as you can see." She twirled

around not caring that she was still in her nightgown.

"But," she said smiling her biggest, "I can be…in say thirty minutes."

"Say twenty and you've got a date. And Kimberlane, I think we need to have the talk."

"The talk?" She was standing strong on her own two feet but in her heart she was swooning, barely able to stay upright.

"Kimberlane, I'm starting to like you." He came close. Her eyes were crossing. "Really like you and I need to know who you are."

"Who I am," she heard herself moan.

"Things can go wrong even when you know everything about a person…come to think about it maybe I don't want to know." He leaned to kiss her on the cheek. She felt all warm and melty like a piece of red licorice sitting in the sun.

He turned to walk away. His body was brilliant, strong and taut, tall. All muscle. His smile made her giddy and he wanted 'the talk'. She knew what he meant. He was a smart man and despite what he felt for her he wanted to know if they were compatible beyond the attraction. He wanted to know her past and her future. He wanted to know the truth of what was in her heart and she wanted to tell him, first about her family and Ashton, then the rest. He had been so patient. What other man having read that letter and heard her obscure ramblings would have waited even a day for the truth. No, James was no fool but to her surprise, he was a true romantic, be it a practical one; and he wanted to know their love would last. Yes, 'the talk' was on, and for better or worse she wanted it, too: to know and be known.

Kimberlane waltzed over to the small bathroom at the rear of her bedroom. It was barely big enough to accommodate the large claw foot tub that set flush against the pale yellow walls. She pulled the silver chain on the bulb that hung over the shallow sink and contemplated her reflection in the mirror. Her big light brown eyes must be the same as they always were. Her lips were coated in muted pinks or matte reds more often than not, her soft hair was always up when she was in public and her nose…ah, there was the rub, 'as plain as the nose on your face' as they say. Her nose was so different. Could one feature so change a face? Kimberlane turned to view her profile. Apparently it could. Then there was the matter of her weight. She was always up and down but now she had what Ashton called a 'mature figure'. He said it was voluptuous, and she guessed it was, certainly not thin but not fat. She had an ample bust line, hips and well-rounded bottom. It was her size and her nose. These features were so altered that she was sufficiently different. So what if they didn't recognize her. She hadn't set out to fool anyone. And now she again had to prove her worth—would this ever end?

Kimberlane was soon bathed and dressed. An hour and a half later she was ready. James was giving her extra time so she polished her nails, a little sloppily but not anything a man would notice. Her skirt was a calm champagne complemented by a sparkling tie-neck blouse. She hoped James would like it. This was their first date so she had to add a little oomph—beige pumps with a nice heel to emphasize her shapely legs—and now she was ready for the bazaar, if not 'the talk'.

"Wow!" was what James had said when he came back to the door to get her for the bazaar, and she hadn't heard another word he said until they reached his garage. There, parked outside, was a spit polished bright royal 69 Chevy with a bed long and deep enough to carry everything anyone contributed. Mike said James bought a new pick-up every couple of years naming them after his mother. This one, the Emma IV, was his only luxury. When Kimberlane came down off her cloud of him admiring her, she considered his thoughtfulness. He had gone door to door in his building collecting items for the sale. And now he was apologizing profusely about making her walk in her pretty pumps. He said he didn't want her to tire her lovely legs. But he couldn't wait another moment to be with her, so he picked her up before getting the truck. She felt like a schoolgirl; was she gonna be James' girl?

They arrived at Mt. Prospect. The large brick building with traditional vaulted ceilings held up with sturdy beams seemed solemn today. The many wooden benches with long ruby cushions looked endless with no bodies to occupy them. And the looming gold cross, suspended by its linked chain, looked even more awe-inspiring with no one in the sanctuary. There was one man, wide and tall Marvin. Pastor Marvin to be exact, sitting alone in the front. She had only met him once but he seemed to be a practical and spiritual man. James told her to go on down to the sale and he'd catch her later. She was glad to go; maybe James was going to speak with the pastor. She looked over her shoulder—James was going one way and the pastor another.

Kimberlane tipped down the stairs in the rear of the building holding onto the unfinished cement walls as she did. She wanted to regret her choice of shoes, but James had called her legs 'lovely'. That made the pointed toes and stilty heels completely worthwhile.

Shelly! Kimberlane's breath caught and she stumbled back into the stairwell. Why did Shelly have to be the first person she saw?

"Hello, sweet girl." Miss Rose to the rescue. She walked right into Shelly's line of sight giving Kimberlane a chance to move behind a support pillar. Shelly was as beautiful a woman as she had been a girl. When Rose moved aside, Shelly's smile faded a bit and she leaned against a closed door. Kimberlane was sure that inside her beautiful caramel skin, she felt puke-green. Shelly's small frame was stretched to bursting with the child she held beneath her plaid frock.

Kimberlane recognized the symptoms, though when she was carrying her own child she had no idea she was even pregnant and she certainly didn't know what ailed her. Her periods had never been regular and her body had never been lean. Her aunt had railed, "It's not the first time a fat girl didn't know she had a bun in her oven bigger than the ones she usually eats." Eleanor's cruelty made Mattie look like a saint.

Kimberlane blew an expelling sigh and turned her attention to the bazaar. Her heart was full of gratitude when Mama Rose had suggested that the majority of the proceeds go to the center for the children's program where Kimberlane worked. Its funding had been cut and the kids still needed a place to go. People were everywhere buying, selling, eating and laughing. Mark and Shelly were close, uncomfortably so. Mark was an attractive brunette star-athlete type and Shelly was so pretty. She had to admit they were striking. It was strange to see how Mark tended her. He was snuggling up behind her and rubbing his hands across the belly of her thin dress. It was easy to see how he loved her. She never would have suspected it. He was whispering in her ear, probably telling her she was beautiful no matter how big she was.

Kimberlane's eyes flew to James. He was bringing in the things he had gathered from the building residents for the sale. He hadn't noticed Mark and Shelly yet. And they hadn't noticed him.

Kimberlane fidgeted with her hands, worrying over the impending encounter. Piecing together some of Mike's stories, she thought about how James had allowed Shelly to go on a little trip to make up her mind about 'them'. When she returned from 'deciding', a brand new element was added to the equation. 'X', thy name is Mark. Shelly wore Mark on her arm like a new appendage with no shame and very little in the way of excuses; it was like she had never loved James and had little to no respect for him. Mike had said, for a proud man like James, it was the ultimate betrayal and a huge insult: totally unexpected and totally undeserved.

Mike had sat on her couch with his hand moving worriedly over his mouth and chin. Like a man unburdening an anvil-sized secret, he revealed that Mama Rose, Shelly's grandmother, had said James was not doing well. She confided in Mike that James had become bitter, wasn't getting out as much, wasn't dating—Kimberlane smiled; she could at least be grateful for that.

"Hey, wife, isn't that James over there, and do my eyes deceive me or is he with a white woman?" Kimberlane's eyes flew to Mark: was that white boy crazy? Why was he trying to provoke James?

Shelly blinked and blinked again. Mark wasn't even trying to shield his remarks. He was probably upset. Mike said that James often teased Shelly: telling her that if Mark wasn't good to her she could always come back to him. He'd smirk, looking directly at Mark who had managed, until now, to hold his peace. This must be what payback in Chicago looked like.

"Hey, Mike, who's the lady? Shapely isn't she? Too bad she keeps averting her face. Maybe she's a backside beauty. Is she with James? Tell him to come over here and introduce her."

Kimberlane's heart thundered. She didn't know Mark or James for that matter, but these would be fighting words if James cared about her. Did he? Thank God he was out of earshot for that last part.

Mike piped up, "Mark, I know you and James don't exactly see eye to eye but—"

"See eye to eye." Mark lowered his voice, "Listen, Mike, if The Black Crusader likes a white—"

"I heard that, Schultz!" James said as he returned to her side. "If I wasn't more pleasantly engaged, I'd come over there and show you The Black—"

"Anytime—" Mark said, his upper lip quivering. Shelly, suddenly animated, emerged from her pregnancy-induced stupor, yanked his hand and dragged him off.

"More pleasantly engaged, huh?" Kimberlane looked up into eyes so blazing with longing that she felt her knees go weak. James was there to catch her.

"Let's get out of here," was the last thing she heard James say before whisking her past open-mouthed large and small women unpacking boxes and laying out platters of fried chicken legs and little squares of cornbread. They scooted by men, still setting out furniture with dangling price tags. Hand in hand, they raced out of Mt. Prospect's arching medieval-looking basement doors.

"What'll we tell Miss Rose and the other women?"

"I already talked to her."

"You did."

"I did."

"What'd you tell her?"

"I told her you were a little shaky, a little unstable on your feet."

"But, James, that was a lie."

"I don't think so. When I looked down at you, you just about swooned," he said as he pulled her in his wake.

"I did, didn't I?" Kimberlane stopped quick.

"What, what's wrong?"

"James, you said you like me."

"Yes."

"I mean, really like me?"

"Yes, and I want to tell you something."

Oh no, here it comes, Kimberlane worried, *you're a very nice woman but...*

"I want to tell you about Shelly."

"Shelly..." Kimberlane repeated, shifting slightly on her heels.

"Yes, she was the prettiest girl at my high school," James rushed, " and when I found out she was just as lovely inside as she was outside, I fell in love. We started to date in earnest a few years after I graduated." Kimberlane could feel her hands starting to tremble so she pulled away from James. He was undeterred. "We were on and off; mostly me. I don't think she saw anyone else."

"Were you intimate?"

"Not as much as I would have liked."

Kimberlane hoped the shadow from the low-looming clouds concealed her foul expression. "Oh," she managed.

"I got most of my lovin' from others. I had a few flings. I wasn't committed to the ladies, some were nice and some were, you know…" he stopped and looked at her, "…available." She pulled away. He took her arm and locked it under his. "Anyway, she was my girl and because she was a good girl; I made myself content with the idea that we would make love when we were married. I was busy running the family businesses and Shelly didn't interfere." He pulled Kimberlane closer. "She wasn't like most girls demanding all my time. Before and after I served in the military, I helped her with her causes: fighting poverty and race relations—you know for a while she actually convinced me that it was possible for blacks, whites and others to live together as equals— foolishness."

Kimberlane felt herself stiffen. She turned away from the man who was saying such cruel things to her. "I get it, James. You don't have to say anymore."

"I think I do," he said grabbing her hand and placing it on his heart. "Kimberlane, when I'm with you I forget about this crap." She squinted, desperate to see what she thought she was hearing.

"Come closer," he demanded, "I like forgettin'. Listen, Kimberlane, I was very young when I first thought I loved Shelly. And when I went to the service my father passed."

" I didn't know."

"It's okay, when I came home I expected us to marry. She wasn't ready. For months she wasn't ready. Then a year passed. I sent her away, actually sent her away. And do you know what she did?" Kimberlane shook her head. "She actually came home married to Mark."

"I'm so sorry, James." *What am I saying?*

James covered her hand with his. "I guess she loved him all along. It was painful, mostly to my ego. You know what I've come to realize, if I had really loved Shelly I wouldn't be so comfortable in your arms now—that's what I think." He moved close, pressing his body to hers. "So I can confess that I didn't really love her at all."

Kimberlane could hardly meet his gaze. "James?"

"What is it, darling?"

Eyes closed, she ran the back of her hand down his cheek and shivered, "I wish this moment could last forever."

"You do?" he whispered against her forehead.

"Yes."

"Will you kiss me then?"

"Yes, hurry." She grabbed his collar and yanked him to her.

He thought to be calm, a quick peck on the lips, survey his surroundings before getting too involved, but her feisty command ignited him.

He was all over her, his hands moving apparently without connection to or instruction from his brain. Thank God they had landed at an alcove in the wall of a closed store shielded from the sun, hoping it would soon close its eye on this part of the world. He pressed her against that wall and kissed her roughly on her mouth and down her neck.

He wanted control, he did. He rested his palms on the scratchy makeshift wooden door and pushed slightly away. Kimberlane's arms were wrapped tightly around his waist, her head tilted in blissful surrender, her body soft. It absorbed him, warmed him and welcomed him. He wanted so badly to surrender— why couldn't he just do it?

James pulled her snug to his chest, looked into the depth of her soul and again covered her mouth with his. Sweet potato pie, cinnamon, collard greens and ham hocks: scents and sensations of James' past engulfed him. He was seven years old again sitting at Emma's feet. His little brother Jasper was floating green army men down on their plastic parachutes near their mother's slim legs and skirt hem as she moved from one gas eye to the next stirring sauces and lifting pot tops. Life was good.

Waves and waves and waves of painful pleasure rocked her. Everything she ever knew or thought she knew flew out of her mind. Everything she ever wanted or thought she wanted was pressed against her, embodied in this neatly muscled, ebony man. Every part of her body and being longed to belong to him.

"Where are we going?" she rasped, being rudely jutted back to reality and the blinding sunlight. James was jerking her along.

"To the center."

"The center? But I want—"

"I know what you want. I want that, too…but I don't want to mess this up." He ran his finger over her mouth. "That's why we're going to a safe place."

James had been to the center on several occasions when Miss Steel had played the reels for the kids: naughty woman…

"Oooh, can we play one?"

"The Isley Brothers?" Kimberlane questioned, as seven-year-old Jane shoved the cardboard album cover into her hands.

"Okay, get ready to dance," she'd sang.

All the kids at Kimberlane's center hopped from their seats, shimmying and shaking. Toes mashing left then right. And all James could think of was, *I'd sure like to dance with you, Miss Steel.*

"Running a juke joint or an after school program?" he had asked her. "The church ladies' auxiliary wouldn't be pleased if they saw you in here playing the reels for these children."

"I'm sorry, Mr. Johnson, but kids like music and they like to dance. So do I. I just don't see anything wrong with it."

With nothing left to say, James sat down to watch. Kimberlane swished and swayed with the best of the little Fred Astaires and Ginger Rogers. Six-year-old Joe Armstrong clutched her hands, trying his best to make the monkey a partner dance. James couldn't blame him. She had the most fluent moves. She lifted her hands above her head and gave her hips a gentle twirl: round and round. Snap out of it, Jimmy boy. This is a white woman, a stranger coming to town unannounced. Nobody knows her and she don't know nobody.

Now she wants to help the children. All of them, why? *Danger, Will Robinson,* he remembered thinking. *Am I lost in space?*

"Put that tune on, the one you played for Jane that evening," he announced upon arrival.

"The Isleys…"

"Yeah, no, hold on." James flopped down on the edge of a large table in the cool room that Kimberlane dubbed 'her center' looking through her box of albums. "Here, this one."

She walked over to the record player and placed the shiny black LP on the turntable. The Farniels' velvet voices caressed her waist as she swayed over. James captured her body with his. Reluctantly, he released her for a twirl and dip. She bumped the turn table. Stuck in a rut, the needle skipped…"love you, love you, love you…" Kimberlane made to lift the playing arm off the record. James pulled her roughly back to him. They danced endlessly to the same few words. When they could no longer stand, they melted into a corner and stroked each other's faces, making silent promises to never break each other's hearts, to never let each other down and to never tell each other lies.

James fell asleep first, laying his weary head on Kimberlane's bosom. She thought of all the things she was going to tell him tomorrow about Martine and E Smith, about her surgery and Dr. Lovejoy, about her almost-husband and about her past—his, too. She hoped a man who thrived on honesty and trust would be able to forgive a woman who had never known either.

Kimberlane was up early. She had found it hard to sleep. So what else was new? Well, something was. Instead of her howling-mares, as Eleanor called them, she was loath to admit she had dreamt of James all night long, last night and for every night since the church bazaar. She had sat in the middle of her sumptuous bed thinking about how easy it would be to love him, to lay with him in endless ecstasy, and she simply became painfully restless. When she did go to sleep, she saw herself leaning over his bed and kissing the tip of his nose or holding his hand as they slowly walked the paths of Michael's Memorial Park. She saw them slowly sweeping the vast floor of the center's multipurpose room. She'd drop her broom and rush into his muscular unclad arms. He'd lift her off her feet and touch his nose to hers. Their lips would meet...ummm...but it wasn't just physical. There was more. A 'more' she couldn't fully grasp. Like she was reaching something, something the God she strived to know might want her to have. She couldn't explain it.

Thirsty and still trying to focus on the real world, she walked into the living room where the sun was taking up residence on her couch, the coffee table and all over the floor. The coruscation of light made her grimace but didn't change her mood. Nothing could do that, she thought as she made her way to close the curtains of her balcony and send a bit of the sun packing. Time to get moving; she had promised to go to Mt. Prospect with Mike. He'd be knocking on her door any minute now. She sure hoped he wasn't getting the wrong impression. Mike was one of those genuinely kind souls. She might have explored the possibility of dating him if she wasn't dreaming of James every night. Thinking about that surrounded her like a hug.

"Kimberlane, Kimberlane? Are you in there?"

"Yes, Mike, I'll be right there." How had she missed the knocking on the door? She sat on her wooden chair and pulled on her lilac Wedgwoods. They were the most gorgeous shoes she owned and the Jasperware angel affixed to the heel made her feel closer...to Him. She walked carefully on her high heels. She never felt totally confident in her ability to command them but she loved shoes because her feet never changed. Slowly she made her way to the door and turned the knob.

"Wow!" Mike howled as the door swung open.

"Mike, what are you wowing about? I know you've seen women in church attire before."

"None who looked like you."

"Come on, Mike."

"You really have no idea how beautiful you are, do you?"

"Mike, I'm just a chunky girl with a good tailor."

"Kimberlane, if you were my lady…"

"Don't talk like that, Mike."

"Don't worry, Kim."

"Please don't call me that."

"No one calls you that?"

"No, I hate it."

I hate it: Kim…chunky girl…something familiar and horribly uncomfortable was turning itself over in Mike's brain.

"Kimberlane…that is your name isn't it?"

"Sure, it is." Kimberlane laughed not really getting the joke yet. "Now let's get going. We'll be late if we don't put some speed on." Kimberlane adjusted the bow at her neck and started toward the door.

Mike reached out his broad hand, clipping her arm. "Kimberlane Steel, Pennsylvania socialite returns home to Chicago. But why here? Why this neighborhood? Franklin High… "

Kimberlane pulled away.

"Little known Kim Smith, just a spunky, chunky girl…she used to live with those quiet people, auhh… Mattie and that man…" Mike pointed at the unseen couple.

Kimberlane froze.

"My God, it is you." He turned her to face him.

Luckily Mike was still enough of a gentleman to hold on to her as she wobbled.

"I knew it," Mike couldn't help erupting before he helped Kimberlane to her couch.

"What do you know?" Kimberlane whimpered in snatches between sniffling and hiccupping air.

Mike looked at her in stunned amazement.

"I mean," Kimberlane continued, "what do you think you know?"

"I knew you were too familiar to just be meeting you now. I couldn't put my finger on it, but I couldn't let it go."

"You must hate me," Kimberlane said, reaching for the tissue Mike pulled from her Kleenex box.

"Not me. Mama Rose warned me off. I thought it was because James was getting into you. She really doesn't want to see him get hurt again. Now, I'm not sure. Maybe she saw…I've got to tell him."

Kimberlane let out an enormous howl. "Please don't," she sniffed, rubbing tissue after tissue under her red nose. "Please don't tell him."

"Don't ask me that," Mike responded to Kimberlane's imploring eyes. "He's my best friend and if he's going to get stabbed, I'd rather it be in the face and not in the back."

"Hummm?" Kimberlane looked up from her tissue heap. For a moment she and Mike were friends again and they almost laughed at his unfortunate turn of phrase, almost. "Please, Mike." Kimberlane whined again clutching his free hand. "I was going to tell him tonight." *And yesterday, and the day before that, and the day before that…*

Mike searched her expression looking for truth in her words. His steely gaze never left her face until finally he relented. "Tonight, Kimberlane, I'll be asking him first thing tomorrow. It's on you. And don't leave anything out. I can't wait to get this story even if it is second hand." He sneered, already at the door with his hand on the knob. "I mean it," he grunted. "Don't leave anything out!"

He slammed the door. Needless to say Kimberlane did not make it to church and she didn't want James stopping by early to check on her. It would take her all day to get her story together, so she gathered her wits and wrote a little note inviting James to her house late. She'd slip it under his dooon her way to the Southton Hotel. She'd spend the day there asking God to help her come up with a way to tell James the truth, the whole truth and nothing but the truth.

12

Going Down

JAMES HAD, HAD A VERY LONG EVENING and he was looking forward to a good night's sleep. He was also anxious to know why Kimberlane hadn't come to church but a small fire in one of his buildings had commanded all of his attention. Little Bobby Kane, as sweet as he could be, at the age of twelve and a half—as his mother was fond of pointing out— was also a little slow. His mother had told him over and over again not to try and cook for his more than capable ten-year-old sister who was out playing instead of keeping her older brother in line. Anyway by the time James got done dealing with the fire department and temporarily relocating the family to an apartment in this building, he was exhausted and ready for bed.

He put the key in his lock and spared a glance down the hall toward her door. There was still light shining from beneath it. *Humm, could she still be awake,* he mused as he walked into his front room, tossed his suit coat onto his armchair and began unbuttoning his shirt. He flicked on the wall light and noticed what appeared to be a folded sheet of tablet paper at his foot. What's this...James stooped and picked up the note.

James, you have waited so patiently for me to tell you about the letter I received from Ashton. I now wish that was all I had to tell you. Please come to my apartment when you get home. I don't think I'll be able to sleep until you do so don't worry about the time.

James wished this was an invitation of the typical kind: a woman is interested in a man who is also interested in her and all she wants is to spend some time. But this was a meeting to reveal a painful past. If this was all there was, James knew Kimberlane would have told him days ago. He would have been able to handle it and they would have moved on.

But James knew this would be something more and that's why he had not pressed the issue and was undoubtedly the reason Kimberlane hadn't wanted to tell him sooner. This past week had been wonderful: that feeling of being understood and understanding someone without deep questions or revelation, without the past—only the future. At this point James could settle for that and for Kimberlane, no questions asked.

Unfortunately the past had a way of shoving its way into the future. For some reason he wondered if anybody had ever called her 'Kim' as he walked the few steps that led to her apartment.

13

∾

Honey, I'm Home

ASHTON PIERCE, ART ENTREPRENEUR and world traveler, had come back to the continental U.S. to reclaim what was his. He had held the promise of a lifetime in his hands, had looked into the radiance of her eyes and let her slip right through his fingers. After all these years, he could still see his sweet twenty-one-year-old fiancée, Kimberlane: her hair delicately swept into that brown-sugar bun, pearl and lace strung through it. Yes, he had stood outside her bridal dressing room able to see her innocent smile fade to a pained line of despair and disappointment, as her grandfather delivered the news. He was so sorry to have given her this kind of sorrow. In fact he regretted his decision daily now. Many are the rivers of loss and unrequited love. There was a wise old writer, he thought, a man, George Eliot, who said, "It's never too late to get what you have coming."

Kimberlane was his. He would marry his true love. She was pure and wanted nothing more than to love and be loved. His beautiful perpetual bride-to-be. He should have been there for her. Been the one to take care of her. He groaned thinking about the lost opportunity. But he was here now; had in fact paid a small fortune grabbing this last-minute flight to Chicago. All he had to do was get a car and get to Kimberlane. He had to win her back, convince her of his love. Together they would save the child. The Steels and the Pierces would finally be united. This was meant to be, and neither time nor space had separated them. Ashton was as sure of this as he was of anything.

The knock on the door had not surprised her. James would come, no matter the time. She flung it open in rapt anticipation to find not James but a ghost.

"So you are telling me I didn't..." her hand rushed to cover her trembling lips and she flopped to the antique settee sent from her Pennsylvania home. "You are saying...you're actually saying my baby is alive. Who, who told you this?"

This apparition, this Ashton Pierce, her would-be fiancé had appeared as promised. She hadn't believed he would, had actually thought that the letter from him had been some cruel hoax. He was older, grayer, leaner. She wanted to dismiss him, to throw him out. But there was still something that compelled her, that bound her to him.

"Eleanor, of course." Ashton's answer broke through her musings and threatened to wound her further. "Kimberlane, what game are you playing? Eleanor was sure that the reason your grandfather sent you here was to locate the boy."

"I have a son…"

"We have a son," Ashton raced to hold her, "and I've come here to claim…to join you and him. Have you found him yet?"

"Ashton, have you heard a word I've said?" Kimberlane pushed away. "I don't know anything more than what you are telling me now and I don't believe you. What game are you playing?!"

The voices were muted but James could hear a word here and there.

"I've come here for my son and to do what is right by you. I've never stopped loving you." She could feel his breath on her cheek. He was sighing at her ear, "All these years and nothing has changed for me. I still want you."

"Shut up!" Kimberlane pushed at his chest. "You are terrible to have come here with these lies. Please leave my home." She pointed to the door. "No, wait; swear to me he is alive."

Who could Kimberlane be talking to at this ungodly hour if it wasn't him? Their voices took on urgency as he quickened his pace. She was angry, demanding that the man—the voice was clearly male—leave.

"Kimberlane!" he shouted as he twisted her doorknob and let himself in.

"James, what, what are you doing here?" She was sitting on the imported gold thing looking utterly cold and not in any need of physical rescue, though the guy was obviously giving her some kind of trouble.

He didn't know what kind of reception he had expected but this certainly wasn't it. Seldom this much off guard, especially since the Shelly incident, he answered in the only way that came to him at the moment.

"You invited me."

"Oh James, I'm so sorry. Can we please have our talk tomorrow? This is very important."

Very important, VERY IMPORTANT! What was he, chopped liver? He thought their talk was of the utmost importance. After all it was just going to determine how he and Kimberlane were going to conduct the rest of their lives. Humph, he had done it again, hadn't he? Picked the wrong woman and gotten thrown over for someone else: a man he didn't even know was in the picture.

His building was as solid as any he had been in, but if her door could have come off the hinges, he knew it would have. He pulled it with the ferocity of a man who was trying to avoid breaking the neck of his unfaithful wife. What an idiot. He'd better go for a walk before he killed someone.

James' steps gobbled up the space from Kimberlane's door to the end of the hall in record speed. He took the stairs, what, five at a time, and he was on the first floor in his immaculate vestibule that Charlie had helped him paint blue. He could sure use a hug from that little boy right now. He pushed open the door and breathed a heavy sigh into the night sky.

The orbs of the lamp stands illuminated his jade green lawn, a mattress. A mattress!? It was sitting on his freshly mowed grass just beneath the balcony. It had to be Bobby Kane. First order of business tomorrow: get rid of the Kane family; even charity had its limits. Second order of business, get rid of Kimberlane.

☙

James, my god, what have I done? "Listen, Ashton, if my son is alive, tell me now! I can't play your game.

"I thought you loved me..."

"I did, I do—"

"Don't tell me that. Just tell me where my son is."

"You really don't know?"

She found herself glaring at him. What had she ever seen in this man?

"Kimberlane, what are you doing?" Ashton was yelling after her, "We are not done here!"

She rushed toward her apartment entry, nearly toppling the small lamp stand. She was out the door and pounding on James' before she realized what she was doing. "James, I know you're in there. Let me in. Please, James, I think I...James," she whispered at the crack of the doorframe, "I think I love you."

She heard snickering coming from behind her. "I think I love you, too, Miss Lady." A wild-eyed open-shirted boy waltzed by her, pouching his lips in a kissing "O".

She wanted to slap him. Instead she slammed her fist again on James' door. "James," she whined as she

154

turned her back and allowed herself to slide to the floor, thinking how horribly upside down her life had become, had actually always been.

"No place to go," her grandfather's voice echoed in her head. Kimberlane looked up, "God, help me. I've been trying. I'm coming to church, trying to find you. Can you forgive me, Lord? Are you real? No, I believe. I want to. I'm so sorry. Am I unlovable, God? Why do people treat me like this? I'm not a throwaway. I'm not."

"Is my son alive? I'm so tired of these people's games," she whimpered into the doorframe. "And James...James, I'm so sorry. Lord, please...no. That's too much to ask. If you'll just give me my child...if Ashton is right...I'll do anything, make any sacrifice." She was soaked with her own tears, "James." She moaned, "I'm sorry, Lord, I'm being selfish. Just give me my son. He's still a child and he needs me. I'll do whatever it takes. His life is the most important thing. Please."

James had done something completely unlike himself. He had gone to the pastor's house to talk. The man immediately assumed someone had died. Why else would James Johnson be at his door at the stroke of midnight?

"James, my God, sit down. Who is it, just tell me." James laughed and lunged toward the man who sidestepped him as he dove into the great sofa.

"I've done it again. Fell in love with the wrong woman. I'm a good man. A good catch, right? That's what people are always telling me, yet every woman I love loves someone else. Pastor Marvin, talk to me or I'm going to go back to my building and break someone."

"James," he said planting a firm hand on his shoulder, "I'm tense, amused and sorry all at the same time. I am going to pray with you; then I want you to go and find your woman. Talk to her. Get the full story and you'll know what to do. I believe in you."

Marvin's prayer washed over him as he lumbered through the night streets. He knew he looked like a crazy man, again: slow walking, wild-eyed, breathing labored: bull-puffs, chest heaving, with visibly clenched fists. "Lord, your son needs you." Pastor Marvin prayed this with a smile in his voice, "He wants your help." James had opened one eye to make sure the man wasn't laughing.

James' steps had gobbled up the eight blocks full of shops, liquor stores, and storefront churches. He'd passed homes and a row of apartment buildings before he got to his door. He knew the route but not because he had seen even one or these things tonight, all he saw was red. He marched to Kimberlane's door. He wasn't going to sleep and neither was she.

Her door was ajar and before he arrived at her threshold he heard rustling. Papers were being shuffled around.

"Hey, what are you doing?" James shouted. The lean man with a loosened tie and rolled-up shirtsleeves turned abruptly. "Where is Miss Steel?"

Still fumbling through her stuff, the harried man snarled, "What business is this of yours, you—"

"This building is my business," James snapped, "and unless you have a legitimate reason—" James advanced into the dark, still looking side to side for her.

"Legitimate, that's rich." The gangly man flipped his thin dark hair from his brow. "Yes, I have legitimate business. My wife and I were having problems and she left me. She took my son."

James laughed despite himself. He had heard a bunch of bull in his life but even in his admittedly weakened emotional condition he knew the lies were flying fast and furious. But then his mind was working better now. This was the infamous Ashton and he didn't know where the kid was or even 'if' he was; and this kid was important to him, real important.

"Okay, I don't even have to ask how you got in here." James took a quick glance at her door. "If I've told her once, I've told her a thousand times to lock up, so I'll give you two minutes to gather your jacket and briefcase and get out."

"You'll give me. Why, who do you think you are?"

"I think I'm the proprietor of this establishment."

"Proprietor, huh? They teach you that fancy word in janitor school?"

"One-minute thirty-seconds and counting..." James said, passing another glance at Kimberlane's thrift shop wall clock.

"I think you should know, Mr. Pro-pri-e-tor..."

Ashton's lips curled, "you are dealing with a world class pugilist." The increasingly annoying Ashton pushed out his chest like a strutting peacock and flexed his knees.

"Yeah, well, I think you should know you're dealing with a man who has had about as much crap as he's going to deal with in this lifetime." James bent to pick up his case.

"Don't turn your back on me, nig—"

Quickly James swerved to dodge Ashton's flying fist. Fortunately for him he had gotten his own pugilist recognition in the service, only they called it kick-ass boxing. Ashton's elite fist was caught and deflected as easily as one would catch a red ball being gently tossed by a five-year-old. Or maybe James was just that pissed off. As he squeezed the inadequate hand, he gave a quick quarter-strength jab to the stranger's gut. Ashton doubled over so quickly James almost felt guilty.

"Now get out before I finish the job."

Ashton looked a little like he wasn't quite convinced. James balled his fists for round two.

"No…no need," Ashton simpered, clutching Kimberlane's golden princess-monster-sofa as he scrambled to his feet, "I've got the picture."

James threw Ashton's case toward the door. It bounced off the frame, opened and splattered papers here and there. Walking toward the floor-to-ceiling glass doors, he let himself out onto Kimberlane's balcony. He needed some air and some time to think. The air was cool and it relaxed him. He pondered what he had just learned…the man was a liar and thought Kimberlane was keeping something from him, hence the need to ramble through her stuff while she wasn't home. He was intimately involved in her life but definitely was not her husband—he was however the ex-fiancé, had to be.

James was going to find Kimberlane and demand her secrets, whether she had killed the neighbor or strangled her childhood cat—he was going to know the truth, all her truth, and if it was at all possible, well, he'd see what was possible…he'd just see.

He himself had been a proud pretender. Serving God all his adult life, he realized that he had never really served him at all. At the church bazaar when he pulled away from the crowd, he asked God for something. He asked God for her. And even he knew in his limited reading of the Word that you had to help God's plan along with faith and works. Not that God needed any help; He just needed to know that you actually believed what you asked for. At least that was his understanding of it. So here he was twice in seven days asking God for help.

"Hey, I told you not to turn your back on meeeee!"

Ashton's words echoed in James' pain-trounced ear as his body took flight: over the balcony, through the trees, and onto the grass we go…

The hotel lobby was cold. Not just the temperature, but the people. Everybody was going about their own business, not caring what anyone else was doing or thinking. Huan, the kind elevator man, had waltzed right by her as if she had not stayed there for weeks on end. He was wearing his street clothes and his street scowl. Apparently the crisp personable façade faded before he even left the property. It had been her plan to check into this plush ruby-red palace until Ashton went away. If her child was alive, she'd find him without Ashton. And James, she needed to face him. What if he wanted to help? Yes, she had to see him.

Kimberlane hailed a yellow cab and jumped in...

"Ma'am, ma'am," she could hear off in the distance. "You all right?"

"Yes, yes!" She jerked herself from a fitful sleep. How had she managed to go to sleep?

"We're here."

"Okay," she said, paying the fare and handing him an extra five for his trouble. She had the strangest feeling. Her child was alive...somehow she knew it now. She rushed up the stairs and toward her partly opened door. A dim stream of light cascaded out and there were a few papers scattered about.

"Ashton! What, what are you still doing here?" She reached and pulled the chain on her lamp stand. Three bulbs immediately lit her living area. A chair was pushed aside, her tea table leaning near her couch, unopened mail strewn here and there.

"Kimberlane." He rushed, grabbing her hard and shaking. "We have to go."

"What are you talking about? I'm not going anywhere." The sucking curtains caught her eye. She walked toward the balcony.

"No," he yelled, "let me." He pounced at the doors. As he slammed them she noticed his rumpled shirt pulled up and over the front of his belt. She felt the frown forming on her face.

"The baby," he stuttered, "I have news." He pulled her awkwardly to his chest. "If we leave right now we'll connect with my detectives."

"Where?" she found herself gasping. "Where is my child?"

"Our child is…is…is in Pennsylvania. I was wrong. Eleanor was wrong. If we leave now we can get there before they move him. I've been here trying to gather what you need." He coughed out a weak laugh, "I can't find where you keep anything." He was shoving blouses and underwear in a bag he had grabbed from her hall closet. "Get a few things quickly. My car's in the alley. We'll go straight to the train station and get out of here tonight."

"What? Now?"

"Yes, of course! Why do you think I'm still here? I called my hotel and they gave me a message from our investigator. I called and he gave me the good news. I've been here putting together a plan. Now, no more talk. Get your stuff."

"But, but, I have to tell James," she managed.

"Who?" he bellowed.

"James, my, the—"

"The janitor? Oh, dear girl," he ground out. "You really have been around these peasants too long. Not to worry, though, I told your manager you'd be going home for a few days to tend to some important business…satisfied? Besides he's not around…said he had to, to fly." His eyes glinted gray, arched and his tone flared razor-sharp, biting. If she wasn't so completely soaked in shock, she would most assuredly have been terrified.

Michael Swane threw open the door to his muted efficiency and plopped down onto the pullout bed, which was always out. It was easier that way. He rested his heavy head in his broad hands and rubbed his forehead. He wasn't a distinguished man. His most outstanding features: his stature, big and his hair, blaze-red. In his mind he was uncommonly common, so he wasn't surprised when Kimberlane chose James. But this, this situation was making him crazy. All of his life he had been looking for a place to belong and now he'd found it. He was head deacon at Mt. Prospect; his duties included supervising the twelve deacons serving with him and being on duty two Sundays out of the month. He hadn't always been a Christian man or even a good one. He started off a wayward boy following the crowd and making frightening decisions. He had reached rock bottom when some of the neighborhood boys had roped him into chasing down and taunting a little colored girl who turned out to be Shelly Madison, the girl who broke his best friend's heart. Oh yeah, that was his other claim to fame: he was the devoted friend of James Johnson and while it bothered his father that he was 'second fiddle' to a Negro, Mike knew James was a real man and the best one he had ever met— and since he was probably always going to be second fiddle to someone, it might as well be James.

Mike had watched James from the time his family had moved back to Chicago. They were in high school together. Every bit as talented as any athlete, smarter than most and kinder than all, James was constantly overlooked for positions of leadership and any honors associated with being among the best at football, basketball or baseball. He was neglected when injured and just plain done wrong most all the time. But he bore it with dignity and grace and despite it all he soldiered on. Mike had never seen anything like it. So when James put himself out there in high school to try to bring whites and Negros together at Franklin, Mike found his cause. James was a good man, and if they were friends, maybe he'd become one, too.

He had no idea being James' friend would also make him wealthy. James had lots of ideas but being a Negro—just like in high school—certain obstacles were naturally in place so James needed a front man. James had the ideas and the money and Mike had the look. He couldn't remember which of them had come up with the initial plan but it went like this: he would show up with 'the face', the 'million-dollar suit' and 'the smile', give a little song and dance about his silent partner, flash the cash and the deed was done. Simple. Property ownership, businesses etc… Mike had taken a picture and joked with James that if their partnership ever broke up, he might create a company called 'Rent-a-Face'. "You know, having a white man give credibility to non-white-owned businesses," he had told James. They had both laughed until they cried and then thought, hey, that just might work.

Mike's father knew he had participated in some sort of successful speculation and had earned enough money to live on his own. That's all that mattered to him. And Mike had what mattered to him—a place in this world: faithful servant of God at the church and devoted friend to someone who deserved it. James Johnson had looked out for him from their earliest days and was closer to him than a brother.

It was this very good man, this brother, who was now in trouble—trouble he had no idea of, trouble that had come wearing an unrecognizable face and carrying a bag full of tricks, any of which when revealed could crush his friend. And it was his unpleasant duty to reveal the whole business to James, a man who held enough emotional scars to keep a psych ward busy for months. What had he done to deserve this?

Ashton had dropped into her life as suddenly as he had dropped out. "The baby you thought you lost. It was all Eleanor and Dr. Lovejoy's idea. Make you think you lost our baby, then she could have me all to herself. Don't you see, Eleanor has always wanted me for herself?"

"But I...I don't understand. You sent that message saying you thought I was unfaithful."

"Yes," Ashton ventured, but paused. "I...I...thought you were unfaithful, yes; I couldn't bear you being pregnant with another man's child. Eleanor assured me that that was the case. Don't you know that only such a revelation could have kept me from you?"

This he said taking a curb at break-neck speed. "Ashton, slow down. I don't want to die trying to get to my son."

"Our son," he corrected. He parked the car in a tow away zone and grabbed her small valise.

"Ashton, I just realized you don't have any luggage, and what about this car?"

"It's a loaner, Kimberlane, and I told you, our boy's life is at stake. I can't worry about trivial things. I've got to leave this place now."

"We, we have to leave now," she corrected.

"Yes, of course, we."

He made her stand next to him while he purchased the tickets, kissing-close and breathing down her neck like a long-lost lover, which in some absurd sense he was.

"Ashton, this is too much. I'm limp with exhaustion."

"Alright," he relented, "go sit then." He let her sit and watched her like she might escape.

Why had he waited all these years to re-insert himself into her life and to torture her with such ludicrous riddles? Son? Why was he here and concerned about their child? Eleanor said he didn't even know she was pregnant—for that matter, neither had she. At twenty-one, she was just as naïve as she had been when she first arrived at Steel Manor not yet sixteen.

Ashton, who had known her since her arrival, took a different interest in her after her eighteenth birthday, treating her like a woman rather than a child. When her aunt Eleanor suggested that she return the affections of the distinguished well-to-do Mr. Pierce, she felt she could do worse. Ashton had been kind and gentle, and after a very short courtship approved by both her family and his, he proposed. She remembered asking him over and over again if he really loved her and would love her no matter what.

"Kimberlane, why do you torment me with such questions? You must know how I feel about you. My sun rises and shines on you. I dream of the day that we'll be together forever." These were the words and the sentiment expressed to her so often that when he made her giddy with champagne on the eve of their wedding, she thought little about him undressing her and loving her. He had loved her for so long; the wedding seemed just a formality.

Ashton—she thought as he kissed and caressed her into submission—would love and free her from her sordid pasts, both of them.

And now, after all these years, he was back. "Our tickets to freedom," he said coming from the counter. He kneeled at her feet, resting his head on her knee, saying that he knew she had been pregnant. She wanted to kick him.

"Your child did not die in that operating room," he was whimpering, "Eleanor only made you think he did." Kimberlane could barely hear him. She was lost in their past.

Steel Manor was bedecked with beautiful bouquets of roses, orchids, lilies. Polished silver was everywhere and gold candelabras adorned every table. A red carpet flowed from the ornate glass double-doored great room. And she stood like royalty in her shimmery designer gown sporting a train both long and wide. Tiny buttons ran the length of her spine. Evangeline Darcy had carefully latched each and every one. Upon her head sat an enchanting fairylike veil, pearls weaved through her hair. She was the princess every girl dreamt of being. Kimberlane remembered the uneasy happiness that carefully flitted through her mind. Then suddenly the great Edward Steel appeared in the doorway. Her tall salt-and-pepper-haired grandfather's suit of armor was a sparkling gray tuxedo. Unfortunately for her his battle was not with someone else; it was with her. "Granddaughter, come here," he said waltzing into the silver and mauve fantasyland. "I have here a letter from your betrothed. Ashton is not a man of his word, after all; seems there is not going to be a wedding. I am sorry you have to experience this but better now than later." With that he turned on his heel and left her dissolving in the midst of four bridesmaids: wealthy thin brunettes and blondes. Daughters of people who owed Edward Steel.

It had taken her several months of filet mignon, more champagne and lobster flambé to put the incident behind her. In the meantime, she had gained a significant amount of weight. This was not the first time she had lobbed on the pounds in her tenure with the Steels, but for some reason Aunt Eleanor did not send her to the country for 'reconditioning'—a friendly euphemism for a hellish weight loss clinic in which ritual starvation and torturous physical exertion were only the beginning of troubles. This time Eleanor escorted her personally to Dr. Lovejoy's clinic in New York and informed her that she was pregnant and because of a hereditary condition, on her father's side, the baby would not likely survive— and if she wanted to survive they'd have to take it right away. Baby...take it...the nightmare-revelation hit her like a medicine ball to the head. She was in terrible physical pain, had been for some months; and now the anguish she felt over the impending loss of her 'unknown' child was unbearable. Eleanor told her it had to be done...after all, what good would it be for her and the baby to die. Dr. Lovejoy concurred as he always did. Through a relentless flood of terror and bitter remorse, Kimberlane agreed and when she awoke, she was minus a child and plus a hole too enormous to name. No, that wasn't exactly true; hellhole, thy name is Eleanor: rancid, infuriating, poisonous Eleanor.

After some recuperation, she went home, ate more lobster, and was eventually sent for real 'reconditioning', which she embraced with a vengeance. She couldn't control much, but weight would never be an issue for her again. Devilish fat had robbed her even of the knowledge of her child until it was too late and he or she was lost to her forever.

Finally her eyes focused on the man, up and pacing near her seat. His slight form was so minuscule amid the ever high-vaulted ceiling of Union Station.

The great hall, as it was called, felt like a temple in the heavens. She peered up to see the dark sky. The ornate pillars with their gold-leaf capitals stood guard. She pretended they were protecting her from this man who was here to 'save' her. Then she spied her—Miss Rose, oh no! Her body crumbled into itself and her hand immediately flew to hide her face. Embarrassed, humiliated? There didn't seem to be a word big enough. What was she doing here putting herself once again under the spell of Ashton Pierce?

Antiseptic, alcohol and bleach: strong aromas to be sure, but not strong enough to cover the smell of 'sick' permeating from missed cracks and crevices of the hospital. The now familiar sterile-looking walls gave Mike Swane pause as the harsh overhead lighting intensified the cat-like appearance of the duty nurse's thin glare. She was sitting in front of James' room as she had every evening for the last five. Mike paced slowly down the lengthening hall, fully expecting 'Nurse Menace' to pounce and snap his head off as soon as he got close to her.

"Mr. Swane," she sang out, "he's awake. I know how worried you and that precious Mama Rose have been." Spaghetti legs pushed her toward him. "Did I tell you she gave me a remedy for my mother's queasy stomach?" she announced. "For the first time in six months my mother was able to go out to dinner with me."

"What were you saying about James?"

"Oh, I'm so sorry," she said clicking her tongue. "He's awake, your friend, Mr. Johnson; he woke up late last night. The doctors say the swelling is close to completely gone. Here, let me get that for you," she slid a small-wheeled table from his path.

"Thank you, Nurse...Howard." Mike said, feeling comfortable enough to lean down and read her nametag for the first time. A few more steps and he was at Room 211 and out of 'The Twilight Zone'. He pushed the silver latch down and walked over to the metal rail of James' bed.

Mike peeked in expecting his friend to be groggy and confused. "James, can you hear me?" he said creeping quietly.

"Mike, my man," James piped, not quite himself. "Welcome. I been awake for hours."

"Thank God. How you feelin', buddy?" Mike leaned over the rail and pulled his friend into a tight hug. James groaned. "Sorry, man." Mike rushed, "I've been here every day and Mama Rose is due within the hour, she'll—"

"Kimberlane, where's..." James ventured, struggling to pull himself higher up on the pillow.

"Let me help." Mike fluffed the large scratchy pillowcase. "She hasn't been here, James."

"Not here? When was the last time?" James turned toward the hospital door.

"James, she hasn't been here at all and she hasn't been at the apartment either. Some drawers are open and it looks like one of her fancy suitcases is gone."

"That's not possible. Are you sure? Did you check with the nurse?"

Mike hated to see his friend so agitated but he knew the truth was coming and James might as well hit this wall while he was still under doctor's care.

"I...I don't understand. We..."

"James, she's no good. You know how I kept saying there was something about her; well, I think she's related to Martine and Evan Smith."

"Who? What are you talking about?" James winced as he jerked his head to see Mike.

"James...Martine and Evan," Mike bugged his eyes and jutted his neck. "Doesn't that sound the least bit familiar to you?"

"Mike, my head is pounding—can you just call Kimberlane and tell her I'm awake?"

"Haven't you been listening to a word I'm saying...she's gone. James, how did you fall off that balcony?"

"I didn't. I was shoved." His eyes fluttered as if remembering... "That man who came to see Kimberlane snuck up behind me. That's not important." He shook his head.

"Can you hear yourself? James, listen to me— this Martine and Evan Smith I was trying to tell you about, they are the ones who had Charlie sometime before Mrs. Timmons took him. I think he was related to them and that brings me to Kimberlane and maybe this mystery man."

"I don't, I don't want to hear anymore..."

"James, I know this is painful..."

"No it's not that, you don't understand...when I was out," James twisted and winced.

"Hey, man, you okay? I can come back—"

"Yes, listen," James said, clutching the metal rails

and sitting a little higher on his starchy sheets, "I think I remembered some things. But that's secondary. When I was at the church bazaar, I took some time and said a little prayer—"

"You, you prayed?" Mike looked up at the cinderblock ceiling and mouthed 'thank you' before leaning in to get the rest of James' story.

"Yes, it's not impossible you know," James moaned as he attempted to turn his gaze more directly on his friend again.

"It's just that I never heard you talk about it before."

"That's true. It was strange, man." James closed his eyes against intruding pain. "I was tired and I just sat down on one of those splintery pews in the back—you know the old ones that Pastor Marvin told the teens to toss out weeks ago— well, I sat down and suddenly the most consuming solitary quiet surrounded me and I felt lonely like I had never felt lonely before. It scared me more than any of the time I spent overseas hearing gunfire crease my helmet. It scared me more than thinking about life alone with my mother after my father died and it frightened me more than reading my first Jim Crow sign when I was a boy in Mississippi. It was horrible, Mike, horrible. I don't mean lonely for any particular thing or person. I mean lonely—to my core—you know?"

"James, are you sure you're okay?"

James grit his teeth and squeezed the rails. A wave of nausea rocked him.

"This is what He said to me," James ground out earnestly. "Love is me breathing life into this world. A man's earnest desire for a woman and her earnest desire for him is my way of replenishing and refreshing the earth."

"Who said that?" Mike leaned in.

"It's that way between me and Kimberlane," James mused, sinking back into the sheets of his bed. "You know, earnest desire. And as soon as I get out of this bed," James puffed, "I'm going to find her and see why she's not acting like she belongs with me."

"If...if you still want that after you hear what I've found out...and when you find her, you ask her why she didn't tell you herself."

"Sure, Mike, sure," James rasped, running his tongue over his lips. "Mike, get me some water, buddy?"

"It's important," Mike said, shoving his chair back. "I'm your best friend," he shouted over his shoulder pulling the room door open. "Remember, closer than a brother," Mike pounded his chest. "You're gonna hear me out. Then I'll give my blessing. Whatever you decide, okay?"

Mike hurried over to the nurse's station where, to his surprise, a very cute little blonde was waiting to give him a fresh pitcher of ice-cold water. As he gaped open-mouthed, she filled a cup as well. Mike smiled then tiptoed it over to the room, careful not to spill the sloshing water over the brim. Using his side, he pushed down on the door handle. James was sleeping, the corner of his mouth tilted—up or down? —Mike couldn't tell.

ॐ

The walls of the hospital room faded in and out as did James while he was attempting to make sense out of what he was dreaming or thinking…

"F-R-A-N-K-L-I-N, Franklin, Franklin, fierce and wild; we'll make your team meek and mild!"

"Hey, Jimmy, there she is; see, three rows down from the top." James peered up above the heads of the cheerleaders into the beaming sun. He spotted her, his Shelly, at least he hoped she soon would be. She was so cute, her pressed hair blowing in the wind. They all looked uneasy, she and her two friends. Pam was getting taller by the minute, dark and thin. James suspected that her constantly talking about being the first Negro woman model to be on a magazine cover made up for her insecurities about her dramatically changing body; and Kim, well, unique was a good start. Her sandy hair, light eyes, and very light skin made her stand out a bit; her roundish nose and very round body made her stand out more. She had a yo-yo body: up two pounds, down one, up three, down two. It wouldn't be so bad if the downs kept pace with the ups, but unfortunately for her, the ups seemed to be winning the body battle.

"I see her now. Smart of me to invite Kim and Pam, huh?"

"Why did you invite them? Pam acts like Shelly's grand protector and Kim's kinda sneaky or something. It's like she's always there, listening. Don't they remind you a little of Laurel and Hardy?" Frank quipped, hands narrowing together and then widening.

"You're being too hard on them, they're nice girls, and Kim would be kind of cute if she would stop stuffing her face and keep the weight off."

"Whatever, man, if Shelly was my girl, I'd try to get her away from them, especially Kim, especially Kim, especially Kimber…Kimberlane…"

James felt like someone had put a giant gong over his head and was hitting it with a ten-ton mallet…goooooooonnnnnggggg! He was momentarily terrified. It wasn't the pain in his head but the unexplained pain in his heart. "Kim, what are you doing?"

"My, my heeeeadd…" James felt his tongue slip and slide against his lips. He wasn't making any sense. Nothing was making any sense. For some reason, he was getting twelve-years-ago-Kim and yesterday-Kimberlane confused. Even in this haze, he knew it was because their names were similar. He tried to smile. His face hurt.

"So all of this happened to James because he was trying to protect her?"

James was coming to. His eyes fluttered as he turned his heavy head against the bolt of light flooding in through his window. Mama Rose and Mike were in his room and talking as if he couldn't hear.

"The Kane boy's sister said she saw a thin man in the alley with Kimberlane. He was twisting a little cloth in his hands and walking back and forth waiting for her to get in a car. When he drove off, the kids ran around the front of the building and saw James laying funny, half on and half off the mattresses behind the courtyard shrubs."

"Pushed over the balcony?" Mama Rose moaned in a worried tone James had never heard before.

"That's what James said." Mike pounded the service tray. "She must have known about it."

"I doubt it, Mike. I saw the girl that very evening at the train station. She looked like something was troublin' her. Confused, angry maybe. At times she was in a daze, deep thought; but I'm sure if she'd known about James, she would'na left him there. Yes, that man did it and she didn't know. He's got something on her, over her, I'm sure of it. She's not herself."

"I don't care who she is. I just want her to stay away from James. If it hadn't been for those mattresses…" Mike looked away.

"How did they get in the yard? James would never have allowed that."

"I guess he'll be thanking the Kanes for being so slovenly; if those boys hadn't dragged those mattresses from their old apartment and just left them there, James might have been meeting our maker a lot sooner than he thought."

"Not that, not yet. 'Sides not wanting him to go; I don't think the boy's ready."

"Mama, guess what James told me. Mama, James told me he prayed."

"Mike, I don't mean to doubt you, boy. But you know how many devils pray."

"He's a good man, Mama Rose."

"And if that was all it took—"

"I know, Mama, but tell me what you think of this…James was actually talking about God…talking to him. He was telling God how lonely he was and God was telling him about the purpose of men and women. Now he might try to impress some people but not me. James was telling me how God spoke to him about relationships. Now does that sound anything like our old James?"

"No, it does not. James has only talked about God when fending off criticism for not talking about God. He told me just the other day he didn't expect God to be able to talk back. I was on the verge of telling him that he wasn't a true believer when he basically confirmed it for both of us…you say God talked to him 'bout his life?"

"I think he did. At first I thought James was delirious. You know from the injury. Then I thought about it. You know, as if you or I had said it, and I knew. At least I think I did. He was actually saying God had spoken to him. So you see, Mama, if he departed this life he could very well meet the Lord in peace."

"Mike," James heard Mama Rose's voice break, "Praise God. That boy can really use a break and to be really saved, well, it blesses my soul, that's all."

"Mama!"

She twisted her head; "You know what I mean, that he's ready to meet the Lord; not that he should do it anytime soon. We want him on this side for as long as possible."

"Mama Rose, if this were true, all that he's gone through with Kimberlane would be worth it. Yes, I believe it. I believe my friend has had a change of heart."

I contribute to the community, both with finances and deeds. I'm mannerable, modest, decent-looking. Mama Rose smiled to herself thinking how James underestimated himself.

"Mama, Mama Rose…are you listening to me? I said I think James has found God."

"Yes, boy, I hear you. I was just thinking if that's true then our James really does have it all." Wiping a tear from her eye she agreed, "As you say, this whole mess has been worth it."

"Worth it…" James heard the words as he drifted into unsolicited and agitated sleep again. He was getting to know God. He was glad. Would he be glad when he really got to know Kimberlane? Why? He wondered was his girl trying so hard to be something she wasn't.

14

❧

Pennsylvanian Rendezvous

"JOSEPH, TELL ELOISE I'M HOME." Kimberlane's aunt Eleanor—fresh from her European tour—swept past the Corinthian floor-to-ceiling columns and into the foyer of her family's enormous house as she had done so many times before. Her wide-brimmed hat flew as her maid, Eloise, arrived to catch it in midair. Without Eloise her satin jeweled purse and matching tan gloves would have simply hit the floor since she paid little attention to missing the edge of the marbled-topped Herter Brothers table.

"Joseph, has my niece arrived? I cut my trip short to see her. And does my father know I'm here?"

"I will inform Mr. Steel—"

"Consider Mr. Steel informed, Joseph." Eleanor's father emerged from the gilded entryway beneath the staircase at the end of the rolled carpet that adorned the long rectangular hall. "I see you made it and in time to avail yourself to the summer party season."

"No cane today, Father?" She gave him a quick kiss on the cheek.

"No, daughter, not today."

"Well, it becomes you. You look ten years younger. So chipper. Where's our prodigy?"

"Away."

"Away? Still?" Eleanor swallowed audibly, "but I thought she'd be home by now."

"Really. Has something happened to cause her to cut her trip short? I sent her—"

"Yes, Father, why did you send her away? You never really explained your sudden need to be rid of her."

"And you, my dear, have never expressed so much concern for your precious niece's comforts. And I had no need to be 'rid of her' as you put it. I thought she might find her long lost—"

"What?" Eleanor flared, her hands flailing, "Her long lost what?"

"Eleanor, your color is seeping. Joseph, quick, help me get Miss Eleanor to a chair. She seems all used up suddenly."

"Father," she stammered, "I most certainly am not all used up. I simply want to know what you thought she would find in Chicago and why you kept her destination a secret for so long."

"Nothing that could possibly concern you. Trust me, this is nothing which affects you in any way. Now let us change our conversation to something more pleasurable. I trust Italy and France were diverting enough for you…Eleanor."

"Tuscany and Genoa were marvelous as usual. The Fountains are building a new summer home in the wine country. Father, has Kimberlane said anything about when she's coming home?"

"I haven't asked her. Have you been in communication with her? With all this concern you're expressing, you must have been constantly checking in with her. Joseph, did Miss Kimberlane say anything about receiving a letter or call from her aunt?"

"Letter! Did she talk about a letter?" Eleanor piped.

"No ma'am, no letter."

Eleanor spied Joseph suspiciously. He hadn't called her 'ma'am' in years. "Father, I do feel a bit fatigued after all. Eloise. Where did she get off to?"

"By the way, daughter, how's Pierce?" her father questioned in her wake.

"Mr. Pierce? Father, you would know better than me—he's your friend. His health is better, but he's still not well."

"Dear daughter, you mistake me; my question goes to the other Pierce, Mr. Ashton Pierce."

Eloise moved just in time to catch her mistress, whose footing was failing her miserably now. Eleanor gripped her maid's arm with one hand while gently rubbing her forehead with the other. She did not bother to answer her father's last question as she stumbled through their red room toward the glittering gold and ruby elevator her father had installed for those too weak to walk.

15

❧

Home Again?

KIMBERLANE WAS BOMBARDED with a tangle of emotions so simultaneously torture, joy and angst that she could hardly stand up under the weight of it. They arrived at Steel Manor shortly after midnight. They must have been expected, Joseph was waiting outside to lend her his arm as he had done so many times before when she had returned from one of her torture trips with Eleanor. His nephew removed her hastily packed bags from the trunk of the Pierce car. Ashton had assured her that it was imperative they leave Chicago right away. That very instant if the boy, their son, was to be recovered. Yet they had waited over an hour at the train station, drove to the airport instead of taking the train, flew to New York then to Philadelphia. And now instead of going on a mission to locate their son, she was being unceremoniously dumped at Steel Manor. Her life was now officially off the track. Her eyes popped, adjusting to the brightly lit entryway of this magnificent monstrosity. Outside there had only been the dim light of the two globe-like orbs that floated above the tall pillars sitting on either side of the mansion. Now in a flash of lightning-strike reality she was back, back in the mystery home of her 'real family'. The foyer was just as she'd left it: a highly polished gray and white diamond-checked floor with a ceiling that arched skyward, columns round enough for a grown man to hide behind and a staircase just beyond, heavy with thick balusters of the most elegantly carved design.

Yes, this had been her home for the end of her teen years and into adulthood. She had grown used to this lavish life. Then out of the blue, her grandfather banished her, telling her it was time to go home, or did he say, find home? It was hard to remember. The whole thing: so painful. What did he mean? Was he putting her out for good or just sending her away for a time? Would he be happy to see her now?

Being in Chicago again with James was beginning to feel like a real home. James cared for her, didn't he, or was he simply another in a long line of delusions masquerading as people in her nightmare existence? James and Chicago, they made up her second experience of home—she didn't count the time she had spent here—twice she had been whisked away. And you know, this whole thing was getting tired.

"Miss Kimberlane, are you ready?"

"Yes, Joseph, I am and thank you for being so good to me."

Joseph looked just the same, a deep dark man with gray close-cut hair wearing his meticulously pressed butler suit with white gloves. He stood straight with his commanding air. He clearly ran this house and had for some time. They all respected him and in some ways they all, including Edward, were like his children. Kimberlane was glad to follow this strong and sympathetic man to her room. She was so tired that she took the golden elevator. Always, she had been discouraged from doing so because every step, and there was lots in this house, was considered essential exercise; and of course you could never get too much of that.

"Miss Kimberlane, may I ask you a question?"

"Yes, you know you can ask me anything."

"Mr. Ashton—what are you doing with him?"

"Joseph, I wish I knew. We are supposed to be investigating a life or death situation and he just dumps me here…"

"That's enough, miss, I was just concerned."

"I know you care about me, Joseph; you always have. It's always been easy to see." Kimberlane tiptoed up to him and gave the solid man a little kiss on his cheek. Maybe it was because in an uncertain world he never changed and maybe it was because in some small way he reminded her of James.

Kimberlane retired to her sumptuous bedroom with its fantasy bed; the luxurious cloud with its already turned down burgundy covers awaited her. She'd sit in her Chippendale clawfoot chair at the mahogany dressing table. No Baker reproductions in this house—her grandfather insisted genuine pieces only. She'd comb out her hair in the secrecy of her room and wear it hanging on her shoulders, something she rarely did in public when away from here where Joseph's people could tend to it. Tonight she'd rest; tomorrow she'd face her grandfather, Ashton and her uncertain future.

∽

After days of not hearing from Ashton, he said they had an appointment in New York to follow up on a lead about their son. She had been in a zombie-like state since her return. Thank God, maids had served and dressed her. Joseph called Zelda to do her hair and she was starting to put on Steel-airs again just like the rest of them. No one was home, her family that is. Her grandfather went away on business and was due back today and Eloise said Eleanor would be home within the next couple of days. Apparently she had checked in since her European excursion and left right out again. She didn't miss them and Joseph made sure she didn't feel alone. He had done this in small ways since her arrival, taking care of her unspoken requests and desires like Mamie's biscuits and Zelda's treatments.

When Ashton first reappeared, she saw him as he used to be: tall, mysteriously dark, with regal patrician features; dapper with a keen sense of humor. He was so different now: no more than five-feet-ten with dull thinning hair; beaten, no more than a metal hanger for his threadbare, once exclusive tailored suits. He was a shabby man on the outside. Had he always been this way on the inside?

She'd go on this trip with him. She needed to know if a child actually existed. One way or another she'd end this, once and for all.

16

On The Inside

THE DRIVE TO PENNSYLVANIA was more grueling than James had anticipated. He was beginning to appreciate the extra week of convalescence that Mike and Mama Rose had foisted on him. He was resistant at first. "I'm not a fussbudget and I know you're a strong man but you are not leaving this house until you've had some time to recover." He laid in her guest room, the one with the yellow and white flowered chenille spread that smelled of honey and lilies. Her pillows were too fluffy and propped his head too high but Mama Rose was fussing over him the way his mother had when she was alive. She didn't have Mama Rose's gentle manner but when he was young he was sure she loved him. The Mama Rose treatment reminded him of those days. 'They' thought it was best he be there rather than his place. Mike, the other half of 'they', was the one who had really worked the magic.

"Remember when I told you in the hospital I knew something about Kimberlane that you had to know?" Mike insisted.

"Yeah, and I told you I didn't want to hear it."

"Well, you'll want to hear it now. It concerns someone you care a great deal about, and the future of this person could rest in your hands."

"Okay, I'll bite—tell me."

"I'll tell you if you do as Mama Rose says and let yourself heal. I'm your best friend and I've never lied to you. I promise you this is going to make your life or wreck it…" He had trailed off mumbling.

They had taken several bathroom breaks at hotels, truck stops, and service stations. Leaving Chicago when the sun was high and hot and driving long in the deepest dark, gas 35 cents a gallon the entire way. Finally the light of day loomed high on the horizon. James had napped at two or three of the stops but was determined to get to Pennsylvania and to this 'off-the-beaten-path location' as soon as possible. What now? Too early to just waltz up to the door. His passenger was asleep so he'd do the same. According to the map they were about fifteen minutes from their destination. They'd nap until about eight a.m., then go and hope the people were up and that the address on the envelope he'd found at Kimberlane's apartment from Steel Manor was where she had run off to. James closed his eyes and hoped for the best.

❧

"It can't be!" James exclaimed as he gazed up at the red building before him, "It's, it's as big as my entire court-way building. Twelve families live there." James smiled despite himself. "This just gets thicker and thicker." It still galled him that Mike had to be the front-man for most of his purchases, no single one rivaling this, of course. It was just easier to let the white boy be the face; fortunately for James, this particular white boy was one of the best people he knew.

James woke his passenger and they walked the large slab steps up to the door. His companion walked close to his hip. "Where are we?" he questioned, rubbing his eyes.

"We've arrived, I think," James responded a bit wary. When they reached the last step, he pounded the large knocker, then noticed the bell. A stately black man answered the door. "The deliveries go around the back and…" If glares were daggers James was sure the man would have fallen dead where he stood.

"I'm sorry, I didn't see you, sir," he continued, looking passed James at the boy standing behind him.

"Umph, I didn't know house nig—" James began.

"Joseph, who's that?" a singsong voice rang.

"I was just about to inquire, miss."

"I'm here to see Miss Steel," James spat.

"I'm Miss Steel." James parted his lips, no words came out. Her eyes narrowed, "I'm Eleanor Steel…you Delmon's boy?" James looked to the

189

right, then to the left. "What are you doing?" She hushed, "Delmon was to come himself. My goodness, don't you have any sense? Why would you bring the child to the front door? I explicitly stated that I wanted to be informed when the agency located him."

James opened his mouth to say what…he hadn't a clue. This game had rules he didn't begin to know. Out of the corner of his eye, James could see Joseph give him 'the look'. The look every Negro child everywhere knew. The 'shut up if you know what's good for you' look. *Why not,* James thought, *what do I have to lose?*

"Come with me, child. I'm your aunt Eleanor. Your room is ready." She turned to Joseph and asked, "When is Miss Kimberlane due back?"

"Not until tomorrow, Miss Steel."

"Good, pay this man and get him on his way."

Eleanor grabbed Charlie's hand, "What's your name anyway?"

Charlie twisted his head to see over his shoulder. James gave Charlie the same 'shut up if you know what's good for you look' to which Joseph added an 'it's going to be okay' wink.

Eleanor—who lived in only one world— marched off none the wiser.

James and Joseph stood silently until Eleanor and the boy were safely up the enormous staircase and out of sight.

"All right, man, what's the deal? I'm not leaving him with that monster," James said moving in on Joseph.

"You're pretty quick, young man. Most people take at least a day or two to catch on to her."

Joseph instantly improved in James' opinion, but

he still needed answers. "Well?"

"Well, I'm glad you were patient enough to wait for your explanation. But not here."

"Miss Kimberlane, please follow me."

"I'm so tired, Joseph. I told you I was returning today so I could get some rest. Did you tell my aunt?"

"No."

"But why not? I asked you—"

"Miss Steel, please." He said it more like a demand than a request. Joseph had a way of doing that. He wasn't like the rest of the Steel servants. He seemed more like a low-level relative, kind of like her. Anyway, why would she argue with Joseph—he had stroked her head after the surgeries and told her she was just fine the way she was when her aunt and grandfather insisted she go to exercise camp, after camp, after camp. He was always there for her. So she followed him through the long narrow hall that led to the little kitchen with its bright striped wallpaper in which the servants prepared their meals and ate.

They went to the little side door that led to the garden where the servants rested. It was lovely; white pines stood like soldiers giving every entering person cover from prying eyes. At the end of the path, wrought-iron picnic tables played peek-a-boo under drooping willow limbs. Joseph liked them hanging low, a kind of hidden fortress. Kimberlane remembered her grandfather complaining about the cost of creating formal gardens outside the servants' section: "All this for the help," he had griped. Joseph didn't say a word. He just looked at the great Mr. Steel and the work began. That was a year after she had first arrived at Steel Manor. That's what they called the house; houses with names—there were some things about this life that even after all these years didn't completely make sense.

Joseph pointed to the burning bushes. Had it been day, it would be possible to see them starting to take on their fire-red appearance. And there she stood. Waiting for what? A shiny moon, ducking in and out of velvet clouds, smiled upon the little white flowers that dotted the edge of the pathway. The gardeners seemed intent on removing them but she thought they were pretty. The stars twinkled their agreement and suddenly Kimberlane felt the tension ease from her body.

Then she noticed them, the lightning bugs floating carelessly against their dark and darkening canvas. Maybe Joseph thought she needed to relax. She rested her hand on the back of the wrought-iron chair and made to sit down as her eyes settled on a large gathering of the whimsical golden creatures. They pushed forward, then scattered making way for it. The silhouette…tall, looming, strong…it wasn't possible. Before she realized what she was doing, her heels were flying in the direction of the imaginary figure. For what else could it be? "James!"

He heard the footsteps racing toward him though his back was turned. He thought he was hidden:

overgrown hedges and tall trees obscuring him from notice—but she would notice. She would find him.

"You're here." He heard the sweetness of her lips between the rasps.

"James," she purred.

"Stop!" he shouted. Then, "Miss Steel," he retorted coolly, placing a flat hand on her chest and pushing her back.

"Sit down. Kim, I have something to tell you."

"You've, you've never called me that before."

"Haven't I?"

"James, why didn't you answer your phone? I called Mike; he hung up on me every time but I expected you—" She sat deflated on a large stone slab.

James shook his head, "Kimberlane, I've come here—"

"I'd like an answer to my question, James."

"Kimberlane, I'm really trying here." His jaw dropped as she jumped to her feet, "You have some nerve. Does your phone even work anymore? I called you so often my hand hurt from dialing. I had to leave, but you...you never even tried to find me."

"If I understand you correctly, you may be the most conceited and self-centered woman I've ever met. Didn't you think me being unconscious was a good enough reason? And when I work up—"

"Unconscious!" Her lips began to quiver, "James...I, I didn't...are you all right?" She advanced. "What happened?"

He wasn't ready to accept her excuses. It was all too convenient. Things were shaded by a web of lies too thick and too tangled for him to begin to unravel. "Are you saying—"

"I'm saying I had no idea," she yelped, tears filling her eyes. James felt his icy façade begin to melt as she reached to touch his face.

"Don't touch me," he managed, clutching her hand in midair.

"You know me, James."

"Do I, Kim?"

"Why are you calling me that? And why do you say it like it's a swear word?"

"When I was in the hospital and they were waiting for the swelling around my brain to go down," he spewed, "I had a dream, a memory…"

"Oh, James, don't." She reached for a nearby tree. "I should have told you; but it was so long ago and you didn't remember me and that was the old me."

"You talk in riddles, Kim Smith, and how did you get these people to go along with your hoax or whatever it is you are trying to do here? I don't know who you are."

Kimberlane bent holding her stomach.

"What's wrong?"

"James." Her voice was soft and weak. "You know me, don't you? Please tell me you know me. If you don't know me then no one can; I'll disappear."

"Don't," James muttered as she reached for his hand.

The wind blew, letting moonbeams illuminate their faces through the swaying foliage. "Please tell me you know me."

Cruelty gripped James so he asked the question which had plagued him for the entire road trip, "What happened to your nose?"

"Joseph, Joseph, where are you?" Eleanor called as she made her way down the winding staircase. Her father had put in a modern elevator but she could hardly bring herself to use that contraption, not here in their home. "Did I hear Miss Kimberlane's voice? I thought you told me she'd be gone until tomorrow. This is very inconvenient. Go and get the boy ready," she barked out to Donald, the servant to whom she had given charge of Charlie.

"But miss, he's just a child and he's had so many quick changes."

"Listen, you pretender, how would you know how many changes he's had. I don't have time to explain every detail of my life to you. I had hoped to spend at least today with him myself, but now things will simply have to change, that's all; now go and get him ready. And where is Kimberlane? My patience is wearing extremely thin.

"Joseph thinks he is somehow higher than the rest and sometimes I even forget he's a servant here; but this is too important for me to indulge him. I swear if he's been somehow colluding with Kimberlane, we'll put my father's loyalty to the test right here and now. We'll just see who he really loves." She glared at Donald, "Why are you still standing here?"

"I thought you were talking to me, miss."

"Why would I do that? You're not your uncle—now get up there and get my nephew ready."

Eleanor's blood was boiling. What if one of the servants had let slip that there was a child in the house; no, she had trained them better than that, most of them anyway. Now to Kimberlane, Eleanor knew just where Joseph had hidden her. He didn't think she ever visited his secret garden, but to be effective one had to have a complete knowledge of everything which could affect them.

To his garden. That's where Kimberlane was. The garden torchlights were just beginning to flicker as she heard the storming of a vaguely familiar voice. What was he asking her?!

"That's a curious question, Mr...?" James did not respond. "If it's any business of yours, I gave her that nose, just as I've given her every good thing she has ever had. When she arrived here, barely more than a child, in her ragged skirt suit, she was stunned and off balance and when she met my father, she simply could not hold up under the strain. He's a very imposing man. She's not the first lady to swoon under his daunting presence."

"I fainted." Kimberlane moaned miserably leaning against the scratchy bark of an old cherry.

"Yes, you did and you hurt your nose, injured your face."

"You didn't!" James roared in Eleanor's direction.

"I'm afraid she did."

Eleanor's neck snapped toward the clarion-news-announcer voice of the imposing newcomer. He was a slender five-foot-eleven: dressed in pressed trousers, a dark smoking jacket—James snickered thinking he had only seen men wearing these in movies—a dotted beige ascot covered his neck.

"My daughter claimed that Kimberlane's injuries were so extensive that plastic surgery was in order." He paused, struck a match against a protruding stone which seemed positioned for just this purpose, lit an oversized pipe and took a long draw. "It was very convenient for her that our resident specialist was on the premises. He's always lurking about, should Eleanor have some use of his services." He blew a long plume of smoke and continued. "It was Dr. Lovejoy who repaired Kimberlane's nose."

"Repaired, you mean replaced," James snorted, advancing on the man.

"It did have the effect of—"

"—making her look white?" James scolded, now breathing down on the older man.

"I am white, James," Kimberlane squawked from her corner. "You thought I was. I'm also Negro…you knew me as Kim Smith when I was a girl."

"You were Shelly's friend. I remember her saying how honest her friends were."

"I didn't lie to you, James. I never knew about these people."

"These people," Eleanor piped, finding her voice.

"Yes, I was Shelly's friend. The fat yellow girl who no one noticed; the girl I would have ever been had not my grandfather longed for another heir. No offense, Grandfather."

"None taken, I think."

"James, you are confused. I can see it. Can you

imagine how confused I was: a teenager who had been Negro all her life suddenly learning that I also belonged to these crazy...I mean eccentric people. When I first came here I thought I was paying off a debt for my aunt Mattie and uncle E, my Negro family. Later I thought these people were having a colossal laugh at my expense. At first I was miserable while I was being made over to conform to this white world, not able to use the name I grew up with, put on a restricted diet to lose weight, made to take voice lessons, diction and etiquette. I felt completely inadequate."

"I certainly had no intention—"

"Please, Grandfather, I need to speak to James. Later the new me became more me than the old. Est-ce que vous comprenez?"

"Impressing me with French?"

"No, just another part of my renovation."

"I ought to kill." James advanced on Edward Steel who backed subtly, dropping his pipe.

"Don't, James, I just want you to understand. I speak French because I couldn't pick up Italian. You see, being Italian, Sicilian to be exact, explained my dark coloring and wavy hair."

James shook his head in disbelief.

"But when I was unable to pick up Italian or the Sicilian dialects, a 'move' to France was necessary. 'I moved there when I was two.' So I spoke French, not Italian. Growing up in Europe explained my absence all these years. Get it?"

"Don't you mean, 'Est-ce que vous comprenez?' I don't understand any of this, Kimberlane." *I refuse to.*

"Eventually I was denied contact with my old family and my old life."

"I never—" her grandfather ventured.

"She did!" Kimberlane yelled, pointing at Eleanor. "She erased all of me! To this day I barely know who I am: Kim Smith, Kimberlane Steel. Do I love…?" She turned toward James, "Nothing is simple and nothing makes sense; and I want so desperately for something to make sense. I want to wake up tomorrow and know who I'm supposed to be. What did God intend when He made me? James," she reached for his hand. He stiffened but didn't move away, "back in Chicago with the after school program and you, I felt like I was being reborn. James, if you desert me…"

"He won't." Edward Steel pulled a metal case from his pocket and popped a cigarette into his palm. "Young man, I am prepared to…"

"Stop right there, old man," James felt his jaw clench. "If you are getting ready to try and bribe me with money…"

"No," Edward said, advancing through the dark, "I saw the package you brought with you…I'm thinking you'd like to spend more time thinking about what's best before you leave it."

James didn't like being blackmailed but he had a feeling they made an art of such things here. "I'm listening," he ground out.

Kimberlane felt perplexed and out of the loop. She wished she could say it was a new feeling, but in this house it most certainly was not.

James knew enough to know this man had him over

several barrels and he was just curious enough to want to find out what Kimberlane's game was. And even though he didn't know Eleanor or wish her any particular ill will, he liked seeing her squirm as she was now doing. She was backing into the row of burning bushes next to her. James imagined them aflame with their full fall color and Eleanor being reduced to a cinder as she shrank deeper and deeper into their cover.

What did this man know? James wondered, as he was ushered by Joseph through a long covered walkway. They entered a distant part of the house that had chairs, tables and couches covered with large pieces of fabric. Several ladies of various races were busy uncovering and dusting. These rooms looked like they were being opened just for his visit. "This portion of the residence is reserved for guests who enjoy their privacy," Joseph explained.

More like for guests the family didn't want anybody to see, James laughed to himself. He was surprised to see that Charlie was already there being watched by a man, also wearing a servant's uniform and bearing a striking resemblance to Joseph. Charlie played jacks happily with a giggling little colored boy, most likely one of the servant's children.

"I like it here, Mr. James; can we stay for a while?" Charlie glowed.

"Sure," James told him truthfully. If these people really were his family he wouldn't be able to get him away from them. There was still so much mystery.

Whose son was this boy? Eleanor's with some forbidden lover? Kimberlane's, like that criminal Ashton wanted her to believe: a child she had had no knowledge of? He did kind of look like the man: what James could remember from their heated, brief and very unfortunate—for him—encounter.

"Mr. James, this foster home is good." The smile on his innocent tanned face played havoc with James' heart. "Can you please stay here with me?"

A lump rose in James' throat. He had known Charlie for less than a year and grown so fond of him but had also gotten used to the idea that their short friendship would be cut short when Mrs. Timmons turned him over to the foster care system permanently. And now by the most odd turn of fate they were thrown into this maze of strange and stranger people and circumstances. Charlie was totally dependent on him, for now. Even this would be ripped out of his hand shortly.

"It's okay, son, we'll stay for a while, you and me, together."

Charlie hugged his leg and James lifted him into his arms and swung him around in the room that was big enough for a family of five. James knew he'd need to get some answers soon. Nothing here was as it seemed.

The children bedded down in the freshly dusted and polished room. It was full of toys, some still in boxes.

"I'm Donald, sir." The Joseph look-alike clicked his heels and bowed. James coughed to cover his giggle. "Follow me, please." Donald opened a door to an adjoining room. It was a rich manly room full of mountainous wooden pieces: floor-to-ceiling book cases, two desks with rolling chairs and a bed facing a great window that looked out on the river.

"Thanks, man." James slapped him on the back and waltzed past. He spared a glance for Charlie who was already asleep facing the other little boy, both having smiles locked on their faces. He left the door that led to the boys' room open and fell into an uneasy sleep. His head still hurt when he laid flat.

Daylight flooded the window of his unfamiliar room. He was surprised to hear the dark wood grandfather clock about to chime eleven. The tenth chime was accompanied by the loud ring of the wall phone.

"Mr. Johnson, a call for you," the young version of Joseph said, standing uncomfortably close to James' head.

"For me?" James inquired. He'd called Mike to tell him that they'd arrived. But he didn't expect a call from him or anybody else. Mike was taking care of the buildings; the tenants all had his number. James had assigned so much of the family's auto repair and moving businesses to others that he hardly had any day-to-day responsibilities at either place lately. "This is James; who's this?" he said, taking the phone receiver from the hand of the servant who was apparently assigned to his every need and undoubtedly to monitor his every move.

"Mr. Johnson," the new but familiar voice intoned, "please meet me in my study after dinner. I'll have something prepared for you there. Joseph will show you the way around seven o'clock."

Edward Steel hung up before James could even respond; apparently people rarely turned him down. If James wasn't so anxious to unravel this puzzle, he would have gladly been the first.

"Mr. Johnson, you're late."

"Mr. Steel, you're rude."

"Ugh, hum, let's get to the reason I called you then. Mr. Johnson, may I call you James?"

"Are you sure you don't want to call me 'boy' like your daughter Eleanor did?"

"James, it is James, isn't it? I've heard about you. Kimberlane talked about you when she returned from Chicago, and though she has not said a great deal, I know she respects you. It's not so much her words but her eyes which tell the story."

"Me, she talked about me?"

"She told Joseph some things and he relayed the information. Ashton's trying to convince her that he loves her, you know, and with them having a child in common..."

James felt that iron punch right between the ribs. "Ashton," he rasped, "that man is not fit to walk the earth, let alone insinuate himself into Kimberlane's life. I don't care if they do have a child...so it's true? Charlie is his and hers?" His voice trailed off weakly. Ashton's character was so lacking that James was sure he was incapable of loving anyone other than himself. "You can't allow this to happen, sir."

"What's that, young man?"

"Kimberlane, she's too good for him."

"Ahh, that's where you come in."

17

Revelations

JAMES LEFT EDWARD STEEL'S study no more enlightened than when he entered—perhaps that wasn't actually the truth. It seemed Kimberlane's grandfather cared about her happiness and saw him as a means to combat Ashton's influence. What wasn't clear was whether or not Mr. Steel intended to put his stamp of approval on their relationship or just to use him for the time being...*wait a minute, slow down, James...relationship? Do you even want to be involved with this woman?* These thoughts ran together through James' head.

"Ah, Mr. James." Joseph was coming down a richly paneled hall in his distinguished servant wear.

"I'm sorry, I don't know what to..."

"Joseph, sir, you may call me Joseph. You are a guest in this house and therefore due the respect any other guest would receive."

James didn't know whether to be complimented or insulted...why would there be a question as to whether or not he should be treated as a guest?

"Okay, Joseph, I don't need you to escort me to my room. I know the way and I think I'll hang out in that garden of yours for a while. I have some thinking to do."

"Good choice, sir. May I suggest you take the north hall for a change of scenery, and when you come to the first bank of rooms, I suggest you be rather quiet as to not disturb Miss Eleanor and her particular guest. It's just a suggestion, Mr. James, but I think you'll find the suggestion rather meaningful."

James didn't feel like answering Joseph. What was this: be quiet near Eleanor's room or was it something else? Joseph wasn't at all what he seemed.

James found himself heading straight down the north hall as Joseph had instructed him. After at first walking just as he normally would, tall and sure-footed, he found himself stepping carefully and quietly as he came toward the first set of rooms on either side of the seemingly endless hallway. "Ashton," he heard Eleanor's unmistakably refined and cutting voice slice, "what could have kept you so long? You will never believe what has happened here."

"Unless you are going to tell me that you've found my son and that he's been delivered to your doorstep, I'm not interested."

James snuck up to the entryway and perched himself just out of sight as she continued.

"You might say—"

"Ah, my sweet gingerbread girl, you did it, didn't

you? And you didn't even need Kimberlane."

James heard heavy quick footsteps and Eleanor squeaking a giddy girlish laugh. Ashton must have picked her up or twirled her.

"I didn't exactly—"

A quick thud. He put her down.

"Listen carefully, Ashton, the boy has been found. Seems some friend of Kimberlane's brought him here."

"So she knows?"

"No, and we dare not tell her. Father has inserted himself. I'm not even sure where he's got the boy or if he knows who the boy is. This is so strange. As far as I know, the man's gone."

"Man? What did he look like?"

"Look like? A colored man...tall, broad shoulders, dark amber eyes, wavy short hair—"

"The janitor."

"Janitor, but why would a janitor go through all this trouble? He's no janitor. Kimberlane showed great deference to him. He may be competition for you."

"I think I might have made some unfortunate assumptions about this...this...did she call his name?"

"James."

"Damn! What else do you know?"

"None of the servants would cross Daddy for me and he's shipping me off tonight. I don't know what he's got planned. You'll have to figure it out for yourself; after all, the boy is your child."

Solved and confirmed. Charlie was Ashton's son. He did look like Ashton—James had tried not to notice it but pretending not to see something didn't make it disappear.

"You've got a right to him," Eleanor continued.

"Eleanor, how has this happened? What game is your father about? He'd destroy me if I got in his way. No inheritance would be able to undo the damage, and who knows when I'll get my money even if I produce the boy."

Just as I thought, James mused. That man was no more interested in being a father than he was in…in…was he interested in Kimberlane? If he was, why had he been away so long? Did he just find out he had a son?

"Listen, Ashton, Kimberlane's in a fog. Lovejoy told her that her child died at birth. He…wait, I think I hear something. I can't trust anyone around here. I'm leaving. Malcolm is pulling the car up for me in an hour. I'll contact you when I land."

"Where are you going?"

"I honestly don't know."

"Nobody should have the kind of power Ol' Man Steel wields."

"What do you mean, Ashton? It's what you and I live for. One day we'll have all of this and more. When he finds out the boy really is yours, he'll be helpless."

"I doubt that, Eleanor, I doubt that."

James stepped off and back into the shadows as he expected Ashton to come right out. He did not. There was quiet shuffling around and then twenty minutes later Aston emerged stuffing his shirt into his pants and smoothing his hair back. It couldn't be; was this man romancing the aunt and the niece? It was telling that he expressed no surprise or distress at hearing that Kimberlane was lied to about 'their' child. 'Curiouser and curiouser' as James' mother would have said.

James made his way to the garden from the opposite vantage point. A small lighted fountain gave the place a glimmer of enchantment and she was there: Kimberlane. The glow around her reminded him of everything he liked about her body, the softness which defined her gentle curves; he now understood why she was so worried about over-eating, these people had made her a little nuts about yet another aspect of her physical appearance. Despite his lingering doubts he found himself floating in her direction. ASHTON! Where had he come from? He was put back together and leaning behind Kimberlane.

"Hello, my darling."

"Ashton, where did you come from?" Kimberlane echoed James' question.

James marched full force toward them now.

"Psst..." James heard off to the side, and a wide hand pulled him into a tall bush.

"What?" James hissed at the ever-present Joseph.

"Patience, Mr. James."

"Patience? If I'm not mistaken, that pretender is about to propose to her. I could end it with one sentence: 'This fool pushed me off your balcony.'"

"Wow, I must say you fared better than his last victim."

"You know about Ashton?"

"I've heard rumors. But let me suggest that you not expose him now."

"Why not?"

"Why so, Mr. James—what are you prepared to

offer her in exchange? Mr. Ashton may be offering her lies but for Miss Steel that is all there has ever been. To expose him now without something real would not serve her well."

"What if I were to tell her about her son?"

"Mr. Ashton is his father. At this point that would only push her into his arms. Don't you wonder why he hasn't told her?"

"How do you know so much, old man? I only found out…wait, you knew I'd overhear them plotting."

"It's not a new behavior. Miss Eleanor and Mr. Ashton have been in cahoots for years. Their constant plannin' hasn't seemed to yield anything worth anything yet, possibly because they've betrayed each other a time or two. With regards to Miss Kimberlane, she came here as a young woman, savvy in her own way. That was systematically beat out of her. Even Mr. Steel, her grandfather, had a hand in it. He didn't authorize any of the surgeries—"

"What?"

"Yes, first her nose, then her cheeks; he didn't authorize any of them but he didn't complain either. I think in the back of his mind he always intended to make her over. He's not evil, just conceited. He couldn't present a Negro—"

"That bastard!"

"Miss Steel is his granddaughter and mulatto; he couldn't present her as such to his contemporaries. I did my best to reassure her. You see, I knew her mother and I did nothing to protect her. Anyway, there are no faultless people here. I was hoping, Mr. James, that perhaps you…"

"Me? No, not me; I've been burned and I'm not looking to put myself into the hands of a woman who wants another man. I've just come out on the losing end of that."

"I understand. You're not strong enough." Joseph said this without blinking, without knowing how close he was to being knocked to the ground. The old man said this as he disappeared into the shadows. James turned and looked on the scene unfolding before him. Ashton was on one knee, his hair slightly disheveled and not fully covering a clear space toward the center of his head. Kimberlane leaned back on the carved stone of a heavy banister. Her face was a jumbled mix of caution and glee. Was Kimberlane so foolish or injured that she could not see him for what he was? And what about him: was he, James Johnson, ready to accept the challenge Joseph had set before him? Did he even want to?

"I feel you deciding." She leaned back onto a large tree and slid down into a chair. "You know why we came here. It's just a matter of time before they find our son. Soon we'll be a family." His words made her heart ache. The words she had longed to hear years ago. Kimberlane felt herself slipping into the past…it was the eve of her wedding:

"The Steels and the Pierces: two great kingdoms united," her grandfather had gushed.

Struggling to unravel the jumble of information she had been buried under, everything but her son being alive seemed hollow to her. He was alive—she felt it now and he was close. Something deep made her believe. She knew little of God but she thought it was He who was telling her that her son would soon be with her. James had walked away from her in the garden. Nothing she said had impressed him. Tears sprung to her eyes.

"I see you are moved," Ashton beamed. "The New York detective, remember him, he says our son should be located within the week. When we get him back we'll be married and no one will be able to oppose us."

She could no longer hear what he was saying. But the thought of her son being alive and healthy warmed her and gave her a hope she had not experienced since that night that she and James had spent on the center floor wrapped in each other's arms.

"I'll see you later, my love."

James was sitting before her; she stroked his face. "Thank you," his lips touched her hand. Parched dry lips.

"You!" she hammered. Ashton leaped to his feet, a question mark punctuating his face. She didn't care what he thought. He'd look for their son. He had his own reasons. She knew that now.

From behind a pale stone statue of a military man, James' hand went to his throat to quell the bile burning there. Kimberlane sat in that baby-blue chair at first rigid and tall, then trance-like, then soft and supple, just before her hand moved to stroke Ashton's face. It was difficult not to gag. His knees suddenly felt the hard cold floor beneath them. He couldn't take this any longer. There was only despair here for him. No amount of beauty and elegance could hide it.

He was going to talk to Steel and see what his game was. He had to make sure Charlie was left in the best possible way. It didn't seem that old man Steel liked Ashton any better than he did. Perhaps the man had as much power as everyone around here believed and could at least make sure that Ashton didn't get his paws on the boy.

James realized what a hypocrite he was. Just days ago he was willing to let Charlie go to whomever he ended up with; now he wanted nothing more than to spirit the boy away from here and adopt him himself. He was willing to do whatever it took. He didn't want any earthly thing more, well, maybe one thing...what good was all this? He couldn't wait to talk to Steel, pack his bag, and get out of this hornet's nest.

"Kimberlane, what are you doing here?" Eleanor popped out of nowhere. Her reddish-brown hair tossed about. "You never walk this part of the property?" Kimberlane smirked and continued walking down the seldom-used garden path.

"You mean the forbidden zone? I had a notion

to do everything I was previously told not to, that's all."

"That's an impudent response—but you didn't exactly answer my question."

Kimberlane felt the devil rise. "I thought I did." She turned and advanced on the narrow woman. "Well, if you must know, I was just being proposed to. I think you know my intended. Seems he means to right his wrong. He told me that he's always loved me and he's beside himself with grief over leaving me at the altar. Seems someone told him that I didn't love him and wasn't planning on going through with the wedding. His pride caused him to flee. Very weak character, I'll be the first to admit that, but he has his virtues."

"Like what?" Eleanor squeaked.

"He encouraged me to enjoy food, said he likes a little heft, and if other men couldn't see my beauty that was okay; it only meant more for him. When we made love he squeezed me over and over saying he never wanted me to change. He sucked my earlobes and stroked my nappy hair. He loved me as if there was no tomorrow. Which of course there wasn't."

"Shut up! I let him have you. Offered you up in fact. He'd get an heir and a loveless marriage and we'd still be together."

"That explains a great deal but what made you think he couldn't love me?"

"He abhorred fat, talked about fat women obsessively."

"Stupid woman," Kimberlane plucked a leaf from a looming tree while her aunt seethed. "Aunt Eleanor, don't you know that when people obsess over a thing, can't talk enough about it, that they generally have a hidden attraction to it? Didn't you pay any attention in your psychology classes? The more weight I gained, the more he liked it."

"The more he clung to you..." Eleanor quietly drifted to the past, "Called you his plump beauty...I thought it was a taunt."

"Yes, he thought I was beautiful," Kimberlane boasted, "I know he did." Her voice rose, "I think he actually lov—"

Whap! Kimberlane's teeth chattered. Her hand flew to her suddenly swelling and tingling cheek.

"Shut up!" Eleanor was wild. "Shut up, you sickening little interloper."

Kimberlane lunged toward Eleanor and would have visited the same pain on her aunt that she was experiencing when a revelation seized her. Eleanor wanted Ashton, really wanted him. *How ridiculous,* Kimberlane mused, *I would never have thought about the man if you hadn't brought him to my attention.* All this intrigue over money and power. When she got hold of her son, they would leave these vipers to their nests. All she wanted was love and maybe with this child she could finally have it.

The parlor or reception room was decidedly more feminine than the rest of the house. Eleanor's touch was definitely felt there. A cushiony dusty-rose and beige floor tapestry covered all but the very edges of the nut-brown painted wood floor. A white-and-gilt mirror edged with a narrow deep-red stripe hung over the mantle of the slab-marble fireplace. Standing tall with her arms stretched out to her sides, she still felt little next to the enormous fixture. It was in this room that Kimberlane sat in her favorite Rococo wing-back chair waiting for her ex-betrothed to arrive with news of their son.

❧

"Kimberlane, Joseph told me you didn't get to your room until late last night."

"So," she heard herself mumble as she walked away from the parlor and toward their elegant dining room. Ashton had not shown. She was not surprised.

"I hope you weren't out alone," her grandfather called from the head of his formal dining table, as she passed the precisely carved pilasters holding up the entablature at the dining room entry. Kimberlane smelled English potatoes… "Come, granddaughter, all your favorites are here. Joseph had cook prepare your hollandaise sauce with a dash of cayenne; the aroma of this freshly baked bread must arrest you." He said this as he raised his gray silver-trimmed napkin to wipe away the flaky crumbs from his lower lip. "And here is marmalade; you know you cannot resist orange marmalade."

Kimberlane felt her brow furrow as she snubbed her nose at the golden drips of poached egg that rolled off his crusty bread, while making her way to the opposite end of the finely set mahogany table. It was their habit: family members at both ends. Very conducive for viewing the river, just beyond the trees and through the large Palladian windows. Extremely unconducive for conversation. This was the way he always preferred it. "No, not there," he gestured after she had made her way all the way to the opposite end of their twelve-service table, "come sit next to me." He patted the chair at his side.

Still wearing her soft dressing gown and night coat, she sauntered toward his place setting. "All my favorites...how long have you known I'd be back?" She heard herself say, as she grabbed one of the three totally unnecessary forks from his setting and speared a garnished potato.

"What's gotten into you, granddaughter?"

"Fatigue, Grandfather, fatigue."

"Joseph, follow me."

"Yes, Mr. Steel." The tall Negro fell in line behind his employer, walking decisively.

"I want you to call the Miss Steels to my study."

"Miss Eleanor is back then?"

"She will arrive at two o'clock. Tell them that I said it's very important—my study at seven o'clock sharp. At about six I want you to put Mr. James in the large adjoining room; leave a small crack in the door and tell him that I said no matter what he hears, he is not to come out or reveal himself."

"I don't know 'bout that, sir."

"Trust me, I'll be alright. Now a little after that I want you to call Ashton."

"Is he at his father's house?"

"He is. When he arrives, go through the back entrance and put him in the small adjoining room and give him the same command."

"Shall I leave a crack in the door from that room

into your study?"

"Now, Joseph, you and I both know that won't be necessary."

"Listen, sir, aren't you tired of all this intrigue. Don't you and Miss Eleanor ever want to live normal?"

"You're not losing heart, are you, ol' man? You and I have enjoyed an intrigue or two ourselves."

"Yes, sir, we have, but after a while it all seems a little silly; perhaps we could just say what we mean and mean what we say."

"Rubbish, what would be the fun in that? Now, you have my instructions."

"Yes, sir, I do and I'll see that they are carried through to the letter."

"Good man, let the games begin."

❧

"Ah my girls, thanks for your prompt response." Both Eleanor and Kimberlane looked at each other. They had played this game before, their father and grandfather fiddling with their lives and playing them against each other. "Please sit, ladies, sit." Both ladies took their respective seats in the highly polished nail-studded red leather high back chairs that sat before their patriarch.

"You are both familiar with Earl Wilson, my legal counsel. I've called him here this evening, along with my faithful servant Joseph, to reveal to you the details of my will."

"Your will?"

"Your will, Grandfather—are you ill?"

"No, Kimberlane, I am not, but I find that a good plan is never too early in the making. Don't you agree, Eleanor?"

Eleanor was chewing her lower lip and looking none too sure about the true meaning of this meeting. "What's this about, Father? We both know that you are leaving your will in thirds: one to me, one to Kimberlane, and one to any grandchildren you may have in the future."

"In the future...yes, in the future. I have decided that the future is now and I've made some major changes."

"Oh Father, please if I've done anything to displease you, I ask your forgiveness."

"You mistake me, daughter—you have been and done all that I have expected of you and I'm sorry for that. But it is for this reason that upon my death I am leaving my entire fortune to you."

"Grandfather, I don't want much but I've invested in a center for children and I am depending on my allowance to keep it going—"

"I'm sorry, Kimber—"

"I've enough!" James crashed through the door that led into the study. "You people are so full of yourselves." He stood between Kimberlane and Eleanor's chairs, towering over the desk behind which Edward sat. "You play with people's lives like you're playing a simple game of chess with stakes no higher than who will serve the next round of tea. Kimberlane, we're leaving here, now."

"James," Kimberlane skidded back. "But where, I thought you were gone. The last time we talked you asked me about my nose and insinuated all kinds of things. Now you want to save me?"

He turned to her, his white dress shirt rolled to the elbow as if he expected a fight.

"I was angry, Kimberlane." His eyes were soft, his voice softer.

"You were angry," Kimberlane searched his eyes trying to figure out…"why?"

"You have the nerve to ask me that?" The hard edge was back.

"It was because of Ashton…" the dawning truth of that heartened her, "but you knew I had to see if…"

"Will you come with me or not?" He looked down on her, his lips tight.

"I…I…there's so much I don't understand." Her hands dug into the armrests of her chair.

"Are you afraid?" He leaned so close she could smell his power. She closed her eyes against the memories.

"Are you?" she rasped.

He straightened, "This is it, Kimberlane. Decide now. I want you to be my wife."

"…No."

"What?" It was echoed through the room. James, Edward Steel, Joseph, even Eleanor.

"Well, then. I guess that's all that needs to be said," James huffed, a little deflated, and pulled his sleeves down and buttoned them while heading toward the office door.

"His wife!" Eleanor howled when James was out of the room. "Well, I hardly think that amounts to a king's ransom but there you have it, Kimberlane, the…delivery boy offering to take care of you."

"You shut up, Eleanor—you don't respect

anyone or anything. James is a better man than…"

"Than who? Kimberlane, I'm not a man. Perhaps you are referring to Father. Perhaps you think this person is a better man than he."

"Perhaps that is what she means, daughter. Let us see. Kimberlane, you have a little something to tell Mr. Johnson, don't you?"

Kimberlane's eyes flew to her grandfather's face. Did he hate her? All she'd ever done was to love and try to please this wretched family of hers. She'd be happy to say goodbye once and forever. But would James understand? "No, Grandfather, I do not. James is a proud man and when he saw all of you pouncing on me, he felt the need to save me, that's all. It's pity, not love. I've never known love. Mattie and E pitied me—the abandoned daughter of a runaway sister and her disgraced lover. And you used me. You brought me here, reshaped my body and mind into the long lost daughter of your distinguished son and brother."

"But you are his daughter?"

"Am I Italian? Was I born in Italy and raised in France? Or was my father a wayward boy willing to risk the wrath of his family to run off with the Negro servant? It took me years to figure it out…but I have one question. What would you have done about my nose if I hadn't fainted at the sight of my white family? I'd only ever been black—"

"Kimberlane." Her grandfather approached her.

"Don't!" She stretched out her arm. "I don't need any more manipulation or pity. I told you that. There's only one more thing I do need. I need to know why, why after so many years of ignoring me did you really come after me."

"An heir," Eleanor spat.

"Me."

"No. The ones you could produce. You see, niece, I am incapable of having children. One too many elicit affairs and adjustments. So you, my dear, were grandfather's only hope at carrying on his line. Your son—"

"My son or daughter...another elaborate hoax cooked up by, you, to torment me," Kimberlane pointed. "How did you get Ashton to go along? Or was that your doing, Grandfather? A way to keep me white so as not to sully the bloodline any further? Eleanor, what Grandfather has done to you is nearly as bad as what he has done to me. The things he's reduced you to."

"Kimberlane, please, let me—"

"Explain! You want to explain, Grandfather? You have taken everything away from me. My old life, my new life, my identity, the man I love."

"So you do love him? Then why did you let him go?"

"Haven't you been listening, Grandfather? He doesn't love me. He doesn't even know me. I'm unnatural, a construction of your will and imagination. Who are you anyway? God?"

"No, but I've been acting like a god, haven't I?"

"Yes, and I'm not dealing with it another second. Call me a car."

"I'll do it right after you hear me out."

"You'll do it now or I'll walk."

"Alright, go get your things. I'll take care of it."

Kimberlane turned a wary eye on her grandfather and aunt, then walked slowly up the winding stairway.

"Kimberlane," her grandfather's voice echoed in

her wake, "I do love you. I've only just learned what it is to love, and tonight I started working on how to show it."

"I hope that's not true, Grandfather, because I don't love you. Tu comprends?"

&

Eleanor and her father walked the dimly lit hallway from the office door to the stairway at the opposite end of the long foyer in silence. "Father, I see what you are doing. You wanted Kimberlane to see someone loved her for who she was and even though it's just a beggar who loves her...I somehow feel she's luckier than me. If he really loves her, that's one, and if you really love her..." Eleanor could no longer speak. She held her hand out to push her father away.

"That would make two..." Edward completed.

"I know you didn't mean what you said..."

"About?"

"About the will of course. That could not come from the father that raised me. I'll wait to see what your angle is."

"You'll be waiting a long time. I've..." Edward stopped to grasp her hand. "Eleanor, I have not been a good father to you."

"What are you doing?" Eleanor tried to pull away but Edward held firm.

"And I am as responsible as anyone for your lack of character but I'm telling you that I meant what I said: upon my death my fortune goes entirely to you. I do this because it will satisfy you and let you know that I do in fact love you. And although I love Kimberlane and I wanted a grandchild more than I can tell you…" He paused hoping, more than believing, that his daughter would take this opportunity to confess what he already knew about his grandchild; she did not, "…even though I wanted a grandchild with all my heart. What I want most in this world is for my only living child to find happiness. And just maybe if you don't have to compete with your niece anymore, you will be able to focus on your own life and finally have the peace you've been denied, for no other reason than having the misfortune to be born my child. Perhaps in time you'll find someone who loves you for who you are and not for what you have."

"But this doesn't make sense, Father," she gripped both his hands, tears welling in her eyes, "I'll have so much. Wouldn't your plan work better if I had nothing?"

"Why do you tempt me, daughter? You know there's nothing wrong with my reasoning. I simply chose to appeal to you in a way you could accept. If I was responsible for breaking you, you'd hate me and nothing I could say would convince you otherwise."

To this his daughter threw her arms around his neck and kissed his face with all the love a daughter should have for a father; and for the first time since her brother left home, her father suspected that a small part of her might just mean it.

From a dark corner, Joseph watched as Eleanor pranced up the stairs as gay as a child rushing to play dolls in her newly decorated room. "What of Mr.

Ashton, sir?" He crept up behind Edward.

"I forgot about him."

"Do you think he heard?"

"Joseph?" Edward smirked.

"Yes, of course, this is Mr. Ashton."

"But he didn't come to Kimberlane's rescue."

"Nor Miss Eleanor's."

"Joseph, the things you know could bury me." Edward ran his left hand over his lower jaw, "Let him stew another couple of minutes, then wend him around a bit and walk him the long way back into my office. Is Wilson still there?"

Joseph shrugged.

"If not, round him up. Tell him we're ready. And don't forget our special surprise. Have Donald see to it." Edward patted his old friend on the shoulder, "You, me and Wilson: just the way it should be."

Joseph smirked. The other meetings had been hairy and uncomfortable, but this one, he was glad to be a part of.

Joseph found Ashton, his suit coat loosely hanging from his gaunt frame, pacing frantically across the floor of the small room, the door adjoining it and the main study now tightly sealed.

"Joseph, what is this—why have you kept me waiting in this closet? There's nothing here to read or occupy, and what of Miss Steel?"

"Which Miss Steel would that be, Mr. Ashton?"

Ashton curled his lip and smoothed his

mustache, "I see what you mean. Anyway, when does old man Steel intend to see me and what does he have in mind? Come, Joseph, we are old friends; you can tell me."

"Certainly he could, Ashton," Mr. Steel as if from a hidden panel appeared, "but I really prefer to tell you myself." Ashton jumped.

"This way." Edward took great pains to lead them the long way, though all three knew that their destination was just beyond the door they were leaving behind. The walk was needlessly long. And Edward kept asking, "You alright, Ashton? You sure? You don't look so good."

"Sit here, son." Edward pushed on his shoulder once they were situated back in his office. Ashton beamed with satisfaction at Mr. Steel's salutation.

"Don't take that to mean anything, Ashton. Joseph, is the boy here?"

"Yes, sir."

"Show him in." Joseph knocked on the wall. Out popped Charlie, perfectly dressed, from the 'not-so-secret' passage way. Edward Steel turned an intense gaze on Ashton whose mouth could not possibly open any wider as his eyes followed Charlie to Edward's lap: "Ashton, this is my grandson." Edward folded the boy into his lap. " I know he looks familiar to you."

"Yes, sir, he looks just like—"

"Like Lyle; you are exactly right. He is the product of a union between my granddaughter Kimberlane and the late Lyle Lancaster."

"No, sir, that's my—"

"Before you say something you'll regret, you

should know Kimberlane is half Negro. So her son, if my math serves me right, is at least one-quarter Negro."

"I have you there, sir," Ashton sat forward as if he'd discovered something Edward had not thought of, "you would no more want to publish that fact than I."

"Don't you think his appearance would betray him, at least to some?"

"Well, you may have a point there." Ashton flopped back in his chair and looked to Joseph for help.

"So here's how it's going to go." Edward pushed a button on his desk: "Wilson, get in here. Now, Ashton, I'm going to write you this fat check and you are going to leave my grandson alone for as long as you live." Wilson plopped a large leather pad before his employer and stepped back.

"I get it," Ashton puffed, crossing his legs and drumming his fingers, "and this includes Kimberlane and Eleanor, too."

"Joseph," Edward looked off to his right, "why is it that people think they can predict my moves tonight?"

"I can't say, sir. I'm a pretty good chess player and I've certainly missed a move or two."

"Ashton, if either of my girls wants your company, they are welcome to it. I will do my best to stay out of their affairs in the foreseeable future. You see, unlike some, I actually learn from my mistakes; even if it takes twenty or thirty years to do so. No, my boy, if Eleanor can stand having a man who spends her shiny new fortune quicker than she can inherit it, then she can have you; and if Kimberlane can stand to be with a man who let her think he left her for—go play in the other room, Charlie—" Edward waited; "…who left her because of," he spoke more quiet and deliberate, "the non-existent Lyle Lancaster when in fact he threw her away because he found out she was Negro and then years later cowardly pushed her true love off a balcony hoping he'd just—"

"You've made your point, Mr. Steel. I'm sure Squire Wilson isn't interested in hearing anymore of this."

"Possibly not, but hear this, Ashton: if either of my girls is foolish enough to take you back—and they can if they like—but Ashton, if you ever hurt one of them while I am alive or even after my death—write this down, Wilson—I'll have you killed."

"Now you go too far," Ashton jumped to his feet. "Joseph, you are my witness."

"Was someone speaking? I haven't heard a thing since I came into this room," Joseph quipped.

"And I am bound by client-counselor privilege," Wilson said, holding up his hands in surrender.

"Do you think it would be difficult?" Edward hissed, leaning, palms planted on his desk. "All I'd have to do is put one of those irate husbands or fathers whose daughter you've ruined on to you and the job would be done. And after I'm gone, Wilson or one of his appointees will see it done."

Ashton gave a nervous chortle and looked about the room. He understood what the three men before him represented. See no evil, hear no evil and speak no evil, at least not when it was visited upon him; and he knew as sure as he had ever known anything that his life was no longer his own. He took the check, eyed it and smiled before turning to lope slowly toward the exit, looking to all, diminished in power if not in substance.

Charlie burst back into the room and sat on Edward's lap again pulling on his tie. "Is the bad man going now, Grandfather?"

"Yes, and you will never see him again. Right, Ashton?"

Ashton grabbed the door, all the color draining from his hands, neck and face, "Yes, but I thought you said…"

"Yes, this will make seeing them more difficult. But a promise is a promise. You'll help me keep it, won't you, Ashton?"

"I guess I will."

"You bet your life you will," he finished off with Ashton. "Now, Charlie, let Mr. Joseph take you to your mother and Mr. James. They need you to help them make sense of the world."

"Will I see you when I go back to Mrs. Timmons?"

"You are never going back to Mrs. Timmons unless you want to visit her. You are my grandson. You will see me more than you can stand. Now go to your parents; they'll take care of you from now on."

"You've done a great deal of gambling here tonight, Edward."

"Yes, I have, Wilson; yes, I have. But I've got a feeling it's all going to pay off in spades."

"Was that a racial reference?"

"No, just an unfortunate turn of phrase. I'm not

perfect yet, Wilson, not yet."

❦

"Mr. Joseph."

"Yes, Charlie."

"Is my grandfather a liar?"

"He used to be."

"Did he lie when he said I get to have Mr. James and Miss Kimberlane for my parents?"

"Your grandfather has used up a lot of magic today. I certainly hope he's got a little left."

"Can I help?"

"I think you may be the only one who can."

"Oh no, not the only one. I asked God to give me my real parents. And one day I told Mr. James to pray with me. He said he couldn't but I should keep praying and never stop, so that's what I did. Do you think I should ask God to help now?"

"Yes," Joseph said, slowing. "So we have you to thank for all this upheaval, 'faith as a mustard seed'. I was taught to pray but I've never believed until today. I think if you pray, you will get your mother and father. Yes, I believe you will."

"Let's do it now."

"What?"

"Pray." Charlie was tugging on his hand.

"For you, Charlie, I will. Where shall we go?"

"Right here." Charlie tugged harder. "Now close your eyes."

"But…"

"You said you would. Now say what I say. If two people do it, it makes it stronger. Our Father…"

"Our Father."

"Dear God."

"I believe we already said that…"

"No, we said 'Our Father'…He's God, too."

"Okay, this will go faster if I just repeat, won't it?"

"Yes…now where were we? Oh yeah…Our Father…please let my father and mother recognize me when they see me and love me just because I'm theirs."

"And love you just because you're theirs." Joseph opened his eyes to find young Charlie standing offering him a handkerchief.

"Sometimes praying to God makes grownups cry." The cute sandy-haired six-year-old boy said, head tilted slightly, puppy-dog eyes sympathetic.

"Yes, it does, Charlie, now let's go find your parents."

"I'm here." James strode up the dimly lit hallway past oil paintings of Victorian era people on either side, large enough to step out and shake his hand.

"Mr. James," Charlie yelped, running to grab him around his legs.

"Does my mother know me yet?"

"Let's go see." James gave his nose a tug.

Joseph marched beyond them. Taking a few more steps, he grasped ornate brass handles to a double-doored suite.

"Miss Kimberlane, are you in here?"

"Yes, Joseph, I am, but only as long as it takes me to pack."

"But where's Amy?"

"I don't need her. I'm only taking what can fit in these cases."

"But what about me?"

"Charlie, what? Did James bring you here? But why?"

"Mr. James is going to be my father."

"What? I don't understand." Kimberlane wondered how James could ask her to be his wife without mentioning he planned to adopt Charlie.

"Kimberlane."

"James, I didn't see you. Well...you are..." She searched for the right words, "You're full of surprises. Were you using me, too, so that you could adopt Charlie?"

"Mr. James..."

"Oh my god, I'm sorry, Charlie," Kimberlane was on her knees hugging him, "these people have made me thoughtless."

"Don't you know me yet? Grandfather said you'd be able to see my father in me if you looked hard."

"Who's your grandfather?"

"Grandpa Edward, of course—Mommy, are you okay?"

"James," tears streamed down her cheeks, "you let him bring a child into this?"

"Look at him, Kimberlane. I had no reason to see it at first but when you really look at him you see..."

"Oh my god, Ashton!" She covered her mouth.

"Where? The bad man? Grandpa said I didn't have to see him ever again."

"James." She looked up. He kneeled by her side and drew her to him.

"It's true. That's why I came here, to bring you your boy and find the truth."

"What truth?" she sighed, then turned her attention back to the boy, "Oh my god, Charlie," she stroked his face, "you are my son."

"You know me. Mr. Joseph..." he looked over his shoulder, "God answered our prayers."

"Yes," Joseph said, backing out of the double doors, "of that I have no doubt."

"James?" Kimberlane rasped, barely able to catch her breath.

"Come close to me," James said, pulling her to his side as they kneeled on the silk woven rug.

"I'm afraid."

"So am I," he whispered at her ear.

"I'm not," Charlie piped, "not anymore. I've got a mama and daddy now."

"And Daddy's gonna tell your mama a story now about a boy named Charlie who lived a lot of places. He even lived with Mattie and E for a little while."

"What, when..." Kimberlane coaxed.

"Whenever Eleanor couldn't find a suitable place for him to be. They didn't know he was yours. Let's sit down." James sat on the circular edge of her round bed, his eyebrow arching slightly, before pulling Kimberlane up on the smooth burgundy button-tufted spread next to him. Charlie remained at their feet, kneeling on the rug. "In fact Charlie lived there right up until the time that Miss Mattie got sick."

"Then the neighbor took me until I went to live with Mrs. Timmons," Charlie chimed, looking from Kimberlane's face to his.

"Eleanor was in Europe. She didn't know where Charlie got off to. She panicked and asked you-know-who for help."

"But he was uncontrollable as usual,"

Kimberlane put in.

"He dropped you off here because he didn't find the package in Chicago."

"You mean me."

"You are too smart for your own good." James winked at Charlie. "Your grandfather said 'he' hatched a plan of his own. Seems the Steels weren't the only ones in need of an heir." James squinted toward Charlie.

"No," Kimberlane gasped, pulling Charlie to her bosom.

"Don't be afraid, Mommy. Can I call you 'mommy' now?"

"Yes," she hugged him close. "Go on, James."

"Well, you-know-who decided since you didn't know anything, he'd do as Eleanor asked and get you back to Pennsylvania and away from where your child might be. Once you were settled back here, he'd look for your child alone and perhaps take an heir to his father. Before he left Chicago however, he wanted to make sure you were on the up-and-up with him. He decided to search your apartment for leads. I interrupted him. We had a little spat. He didn't like the way it turned out so when I turned my back on him and went out to the balcony for air, he decided I needed to learn how to fly. It took me weeks to wake up from the lesson."

"James, you could have…"

"And now I know why you didn't come to see about me."

"James," Kimberlane shook her head violently and placed a trembling hand on his temple, "I didn't know."

James clasped her fingers, "I know. I know now why you didn't come." He kissed her hand.

Charlie smiled. "Don't worry. We have each other now. I'm sleepy. Can we go to bed now? Together?" He smiled up at them.

"I'm not sure that's a good..." Kimberlane rambled, getting nervously to her feet.

"Kimberlane, aren't you tired of being alone?" James stood, following her. "It's only sleep. Let's give our son what he wants. After tomorrow it won't matter."

"Alright," Kimberlane agreed, surprising James.

"Yippee! I'll go get my pajamas!"

"All the way in the guest house?" James' voice echoed across the large room.

"No, I have some in Grandpa's room." Charlie raced to the door. "I'll be right back."

"James, should we be doing this?" Kimberlane asked, moving quickly to close the door behind him.

"We're just sleeping," James crossed a vast chasm of carpets, tapestries, hulking dressers and claw foot thrones to move to her side, "and as I said, tomorrow it won't matter."

"I know you did," Kimberlane whispered. "James," she stepped back arching her head so she could read his bright eyes, "what did you mean by that?"

"I meant," James advanced pulling her arms around his waist, "tomorrow or the earliest day after that, I intend to have you for my wife and to never ever look back."

"What if I'm not black?" She was pinned against the wall and looking straight up now.

"Don't you mean what if you are?" He pulled the

pins from her hair and ran his fingers through. "I've only really known you as a white woman. Hey…that's why you wore your hair up all the time. You were worried someone might notice that…" he buried his face in the waves and breathed in. "I barely knew you in high school before you left and these people got a hold of you. Knowing them better gives me a big clue as to why you were so confused."

"But I…"

"Kimberlane, I don't care what you are anymore…Negro, white, mulatto. All I care is that you are…my wife and the mother of my children."

"You want to have children with me? But what will they be?"

"You mean besides human and ours…"

"You know what I mean." He was pressing the air out of her and her good sense, too.

"Do you love me, Kimberlane?"

"You're making it hard for me to think." She squirmed, the thick wainscoting molding pressing into her back.

"It's a simple question." He nibbled her ear.

"I don't think we should sleep together."

"You'll be on one side. I'll be on the other. Charlie will be in the middle. Now answer the question. I already know you have the h…"

"Yes, yes, I love you." She shoved him lightly.

"Then Charlie wasn't the only one who had his prayers answered tonight." He eyed her mischievously. "Now give me a kiss before our son gets back and we have to 'just' sleep in the same bed."

Kimberlane, still disheveled, stepped to him and pressed her parted lips to his. Their bodies because instantly wound.

The softness of her kiss against the firmness of his grasp brought back memories of their unfinished business. "I'm sleeping on the floor," James groaned.

"No, I'll stop," Kimberlane whimpered, not stopping, "we promised our son."

Lost in each other's embrace, only Charlie's yell could rouse them. "This is like a dream!" he roared. James turned, his outstretched arms opening just in time to catch Charlie flying into them.

"A dream come true." Kimberlane rushed, hurling them all toward the thick fluffiness of her imported round bed. They rolled into the huge marshmallow pillows, laughing hysterically and holding onto each other as if their very lives depended on it—and they did.

Eleanor awoke to a dark room but inside she felt light. She immediately flipped the smooth purple coverlet off her canopy bed and rushed to her crystal-white dresser.

"Where is it?" she mumbled, while shuffling through the papers in her top drawer. "Here," she sighed, pressing the crinkled photo to her chest, "David."

Suddenly memories as sweet as Dutch chocolate and whipped cream flooded her mind. She and David were running through the grand halls of the manor unaware that there were people in the world who didn't have bright orange marmalade that stuck to their fingers as they slathered it on soft warm bread for breakfast each morning. Children everywhere sock-skied on marble floors long and wide enough to zip up one end and down the other without bumping into a thing. Didn't every kid have servants waiting behind limestone pillars to pick up their yarn-haired, button-eyed, stuffed Raggedy Ann dolls or bring them their toy soldier nutcrackers? This was the world of Eleanor and David.

She adored her beautiful brother and he doted on her. They spent hours frolicking in the gardens and days skipping up the stairs and sliding down the spiral banisters. "David." She looked again at the fading photo of her brother, holding her hand and smiling down at her. She was content with the world and so was he; that was until he was about ten and started to notice that the servant kids were not having as much fun as they were. In fact they only got to play when their parents didn't need their help and there were no 'outside' people visiting.

"Why can't my house-friends play with my visiting friends?" he'd ask Ann, their mother. "They're not your friends, son. They are your servants. There is a difference." But David didn't see it that way. He never would. He started brooding. "I want Donald to come to my party." He insisted when he was eleven.

"He'll be there, David."

"As a friend?"

"No, not as a friend. I've explained this to you. He can come as a servant."

"I don't like it, Mother." But he ate giant hunks of his frosted cake and he licked all the lollipop flavors, he rode his new bike right in the house and played horseshoes on the lawn, all while Donald and Willie stood in the thick grass wearing their neat blue knee suits, crisp white shirts and bowties, holding trays of potato chips and sausage with pitchers of ice cold lemonade made by their mothers. He jumped, skipped, laughed and hid but after the party he was not the same. He didn't play with Donald and Willie. He hardly played with her. He refused to go into town with his father and he slighted his mother.

When he was nineteen he packed his bags.

"Come with me, Eleanor," he grabbed her by the hand. "I want to talk to you." They walked out into the bright sunshine off into the heavy woods that bordered their home. "I have to tell you something," he warned, averting his hazel eyes while locking his arm and hers.

"What is it, David?" she said, impatient to be done and getting ready for her tea party. "I'm leaving Steel Manor."

"Yes, and when will you be back?"

"I'm not coming back, Eleanor."

"You're silly, David. Where will you live?"

"Not here. I can't stay here." He pulled her down to sit on a stone bench by the simmering pool in their hedge garden.

"David, please stop joking. I have to have Sally hem the lace on my new flare skirt." She'd kissed his cheek and rose to follow the stone path that had taken them there. "Wait," he said raising to his feet, "perhaps I will see you again, but if I don't I want to know you have been the best sister a boy...I mean a man could ever have, and I love you."

"And you are a very silly brother. I'll see you

tonight." She ran back up the path as happy as a lark to put on her new outfit and greet her friends. If she had only known that this was the last time she'd ever see her brother, she would have hugged his neck and never let him go.

Viola, a young servant was starting to show. Everyone assumed the child was Donald's. She was allowed to stay since Donald was Joseph's nephew and no one dared cross Joseph. It was also assumed, and Ann would see to it, that in another month before Viola got any bigger, Donald would marry her. Donald never got the chance. On the day David disappeared so did Viola. After months of looking for David, Ann died of a broken heart. Not able to save his wife, Edward gave up the search, understanding that finding the son also meant finding the colored grandchild. His loss became a bitter vine, twisting and churning the life out of the remaining child—her.

But today she could look at her brother and smile. Today she could love him again, because maybe, just maybe, her father loved her. She kissed David's picture and propped it by the Oriental vase. David was no more, but Kimberlane was alive. His daughter, who for some reason she no longer hated, lay just beyond the unassuming paneled door that adjoined their rooms. But it wasn't respectful to simply barge in. She'd go around and enter through the double doors. She'd be an invited guest rather than an intruding aunt.

Eleanor carefully removed the foam rollers from her hair and pinched color into her cheeks. She pulled her lacy teal robe from the blanket bench at the foot of her bed and strolled across the expanse of her seashell-peach room toward the opaque stained-glass doors that led to the hall. Her heeled slippers made small clicking sounds as her steps carried her to the room of her niece. "Kimberlane," she hissed just above a whisper, fingering the hand carving on the slightly parted entry.

"Uhhh…"

The groan was unfamiliar. "Who?" Eleanor shoved the solid mahogany doors, totally unprepared for the sight before her.

"What, umm…" There on her fanciful Italian bed lay Kimberlane, still wearing the ivory and plum shift she had on last night. Her arm was draped around the boy she now knew to be her nephew. He had changed into shocking-orange Woody Woodpecker pajamas. Both were firmly anchored by James Johnson's sinewy right arm. He had taken the time to remove the imported cotton shirt which he had most likely borrowed from their peacock servant Donald. But James wore it so much better. She could admit it now—this was no landlord or delivery boy; he was no shiftless soldier either. Before her lay a general having the same bearing as Joseph. She could see now what her brother was able to see eons ago. Some of them are as good as some of us. Eleanor contemplated the sight before her. She could almost envy her niece—almost.

It was time. She'd tell Kimberlane everything tomorrow. She closed her eyes and turned from the sight of the circular bed and its inhabitants and started for the door.

"Eleanor," a voice like strong cognac thundered.

"Yes," she turned, unable to control the subtle tremble that came over her.

"You gotta tell me what I'm dealin' with here."

"What, I...I...don't understand." Her voice was quavering. She didn't like it.

"I was saying, I need to talk to you." The demand was unmistakable.

" I...what I have to say is for Kimberlane. I owe her an explanation."

"You sure do."

He was up and giving her arm a gentle tug. She couldn't meet his gaze. Her eyes flew to his muscular chest. He noticed, then grabbed and replaced his shirt in one fluid motion. "From what I can gather, you've given one blow after another to my woman."

"Your woman?"

"Yes, my woman. And nothing else I can see comin' is ever going to hurt her again. So I'm telling you that anything else you have to say to her is going through me first. You've done her enough harm to last a lifetime."

"I have..."

"You have; but you know that."

"I do and you're right. I've come here to confess my sins. I love my brother David and the pain I felt at his desertion was unbearable. And when my mother died, my father became aloof...I'm sorry...aloof—"

"I know what it means, go on..."

Eleanor looked around the cavernous suite at Kimberlane's furnishings. Baroque tapestries, she had picked. Golden candlesticks she had placed, trying to make sure her presence was felt even here. "It was as if I didn't exist. James, that's your name right? Do you have any idea how it feels to be deserted by the only person who really loves you?"

"I have some idea."

"Have you? Then you understand my pain. I was a child. My brother was gone. My mother was gone. And the one person who was supposed to help me to get through the loss didn't want me anymore. I was so desperate."

"Arrrr," Kimberlane groaned, her fingers arching to pull Charlie to her bosom.

"Let's move this outside," James demanded, grabbing the grand doors by their handles.

"Thank you," Eleanor offered as he pulled out the Chippendale in the alcove near the floor-to-ceiling windows at the end of the hall. James stood staring out over hill after hill of lush grass in one direction, tall forest beyond gardens in another, and a fast-flowing river in yet another.

"Beautiful, isn't it?"

"Yes, it is. I've seen stuff like this in movies. To think people actually live like this…it's amazing." James smiled despite himself.

"You don't speak like—"

"Like what, a Negro, an uneducated—?"

"Like a janitor…"

"That's probably because I'm not, Miss Steel, I own the place. And while I don't see ever owning a place like this, I do have the means to support your niece nicely. Now, let's get to the point. I need you to tell me what I'm up against. What have you and your father done to her that I'm going to have to undo."

"Well put, Mr. James. We have damaged her. Mostly me, and I am, only now, beginning to feel some regret."

18

෧

Man To Man

EDWARD SPIED THE CONFUSED and agitated
Joseph as he walked into his master bedroom suite.
He knew Joseph, and Joseph knew him. Edward
knew his concern, so he was not surprised when
Joseph straightened his face and started right in. "You
think she'll be happy living modestly?"

"She's lived with poverty. She's lived with great
wealth. She'll be happy with James. Besides, she can
live any way she wants and on his money for a
change."

"His money?"

"That boy is loaded. He owns three apartment
buildings, a car repair business, and a moving and
storage business, and that does not include the life
insurance policy money he received when the elder
Johnsons died."

"Anything else, sir?" Joseph quipped as he placed

Edward Steel's tea on the teak wood table and snapped the napkin he had draped across his arm before placing it on his employer's lap.

"I stopped the investigation when I knew she'd be taken care of." Edward sipped his tea, "it's not my fortune but it'll do; and do you think I would have let her go to a man who couldn't support her in the style to which she has become accustomed?"

"Have you told her about the money her kids will inherit from your wife's people?"

"Plenty of time for that; I think she's had enough revelations. Besides I just found out about the money myself. When Wilson discovered that there was no particular stipulation in my wife's will that David's children had to have resulted from a legal marriage, he confirmed that Kimberlane and her children were entitled to at least half of Ann's family money. As you know it was entailed to her heirs upon the birth of their children. Her family was obsessed with legacy."

"More than yours, sir?"

"That's good, Joseph, very good. But as you see that leaves only Kimberlane. David ran off with Kimberlane's mother and disappeared, leaving Kimberlane with Mattie. He was afraid they'd never have any peace if my granddaughter was missing. I'd never leave him alone if he had the only means for continuing my bloodline, Negro or not. And poor Eleanor never having any children didn't qualify. I never told her about the money...salt in the wound, you know. Ann's family was very vain. They wanted to make sure that their lineage would be here as long as time itself. Anyway we've had enough revelations for the time being."

"For a lifetime, sir, for a lifetime."

19

Enough!

DIZZY, CAN'T SEE STRAIGHT, CRAZY MAD. James glared up into the square-tiled, quietly etched, flower-petal ceiling, willing himself to be as far away from Eleanor as possible. He didn't want to kill her. He asked himself, who, who could imagine and perpetrate such grotesque intrigue?

Kimberlane, a depressed overweight twenty-one-year-old, was taken to the family physician's private clinic, doubled over with pain she didn't understand.

"What's happening, Aunt?" Kimberlane had asked, using both her delicate hands to clutch her tightening abdomen. "Dr. Lovejoy has cancelled all his patients for us. He should be here soon. Stop whining," was Eleanor's 'sympathetic' reply before she demanded that she and her niece to be escorted from the brightly lit and very crowded waiting room into the doctor's elegantly apportioned private examining room, containing a mahogany bar, a satin-sheeted bed and enough equipment and medical supplies to discreetly perform any operation right then and there.

"Aunt Eleanor, it hurts so much!" Kimberlane clutched her arm so hard she dug half-moons into her wrists. She'd felt a little sorry for Kimberlane. But she didn't let that change her plans. She needed to weaken her niece, to control her, and she certainly could not have another illegitimate heir being raised to compete for their fortune. "Kimberlane, Dr. Lovejoy says the baby is not going to make it and neither are you."

"Baby!" Kimberlane squealed, "I'm having a baby!"

"You have to let the doctor take it."

Eleanor explained how she ignored Kimberlane's questions, pressing her point before she lost her nerve: "It'll die quick. And maybe you'll live if we do it now." James heard Eleanor's voice catch as she relayed this bit of treachery. "You don't want the baby to be born and suffer for hours before it eventually dies anyway. Kimberlane, if you love this baby you'll let it go." James held his trembling hands up to his face. He saw himself crushing Eleanor's throat. Her tears caused him to hesitate. "I really am sorry about that," she continued, her back turned to him, gazing out of the windows. She forced Kimberlane to decide to end the child's life, assuring that she alone would feel the responsibility of that decision. After sending the live 'unaborted' baby to a Catholic-run high-end orphanage for his first four years, she paid a high-ranking Illinois official to orchestrate a number of foster placements. She even allowed him to stay with Mattie and E a couple of times. A kind of test to see if they'd recognize him. That backfired. When Eleanor was in Europe, her hired gun was fired; Mattie died and the boy was lost track of. For a while Eleanor didn't concern herself with that small detail. That was until her father learned she could not have children, making Kimberlane and her children, or lack thereof, of prime importance to them both. Eleanor needed to control events again. Ashton also in need of an heir—seems he could only sire one—became her partner in crime. Together they would find Kimberlane's son and use him in whatever way seemed best. If they could manage not to betray each other in the process. Turns out that was a big 'if'.

Eleanor rose from the ornate gold-and-bronze-colored chair, light and flighty, prancing wildly as if years' worth of burden had suddenly been relieved from her shoulders. "Wait," James piped as she floated away, "did Ashton actually think Kimberlane had been unfaithful to him? Is that why he called off the marriage?"

"Who said that?"

"Apparently you did."

"Did he tell you that? My dear Ashton, always something new. I didn't tell him that. I would not. It was my father's plan that they should be married and at that time I wouldn't dare betray him. It was not me. Ashton left Kimberlane on their wedding day because on the morning of their wedding he was told that Kimberlane was half Negro."

"You told him—"

"Not me. I don't know who did; but if I had to guess…my bet would be Joseph. Probably thought she was too good for him and when no miracle happened to put a wedge between them, he intervened. Of course this is all speculation, but he's the only one I know with the guts to do such a thing. Well, that's all the good I can muster. Goodbye, Mr. James. I really don't care to see you again."

James sat, the sun blistering him through the opaque sapphire and gold glass. Eleanor pranced away in her elegant robe and high-heeled slippers, the gruesome boulder rolling right off her slender shoulders and on to his. He smiled. Fortunately he was not alone. A new sensation arose. He had every intention of taking it to the Lord, as the old people used to say. He didn't know exactly how he'd do it, but seeing as it had worked so well in getting Kimberlane back and bringing him and Charlie together, it was certainly worth a try.

$\mathcal{E}$pilogue

Time Heals

"WHAT'S THIS, SIR?" Joseph questioned, entering the massive bedroom of Edward Steel, the mastermind behind as many failed ventures as he had successful ones in steel, coal, various other enterprises and multiple intrigues. His room like his home had prized acquisitions from tantalizing Argentina to mythic Egypt. It was comfortable but daunting; many a man, even those as rich as his employer, might have been intimidated by the overpowering enormity of it all.

"I'm going to Chicago."

Joseph had become used to this salutation. Ever since the showdown—years ago—his employer, the great Edward Steel, traveled frequently to the Windy City.

"And you packed your own bags?" Joseph said,

looking about the room at suit pants over the backs of shield chairs, pressed shirts on the Oriental rug, drunken toiletries strewn this way and that and suitcases with clothing items cinched into zippers, half in, half out.

"Yes, I'm a grown man; I should be able to do it, don't you think?"

"Of course, of course you should." Joseph's lips strained for composure.

"I packed yours, too."

"Oh no."

"Oh yes. Vacation. I'm taking another."

"And you want me to accompany you?"

"No, I want you to take care of yourself for a change."

"You are going to see Mrs. Johnson then."

"Yes, the boys are getting big and as they say 'three is a charm.' We're hoping for a girl this time. At any rate, I intend to be there when it happens."

"Sir, I have to say a change has come over you."

"Not as big a change as I'm hoping for."

"I don't understand."

"The kids tell me there's a lady named Rose who's got the whole lot of them in church. I used to be man of the Word."

"I know. You read the Good Book and take an interest in religions of all kinds. I didn't think the Lord's book meant anything more to you than the rest."

"Joseph, I read the Quran, the Torah, the Bible and many others; what needles me is that the first three all deal with Christ. Why is that? One day I stopped studying and I said a sort of prayer. I simply said, 'Christ Jesus, if you are God make it known to me.' I realized like a bolt of lightning that all these faiths dealt with him because He had to be dealt with. The religions that didn't acknowledge Him as Lord knew He could not be ignored so that sought to minimize Him. Why bother, I asked myself?"

"Why indeed." Joseph mimicked, in wide-eyed amazement, arms folded, taking in the amount of work it would take to reconstruct this bedroom.

Joseph knew Edward to be no more a Christian than he was, so he was taken aback by the next question, "Joseph, have you ever read Revelation?"

"You know, sir, it's the kind of...I mean...I've been meaning to—"

"Don't bother. After the first three chapters, I nearly soiled myself. It's not a fit place for the ungodly to venture."

"I see why you quit it, sir."

"That's why I like you, Joseph."

"No, sir, that's not the reason. You like me because I keep your secrets."

"Yes, there is that. I don't believe there'll be much need for those kinds of services in the future. I studied the scripture but, as the Johnsons say, I didn't know the Lord. Like that thing with the demons—"

"What thing, sir?"

"That thing, in the Bible, about them trembling but not changing."

"That bothered you."

"It resembled me. Joseph, I'm not getting any younger and the older you get, the closer you get to..." Edward Steel pointed his finger toward the endless space that led to the ceiling. "I figure I've spent years at arms' length and it's about time I got close enough to touch before it's too late. So go anywhere you want, on me, and when you come back you have the run of the place."

"Me, sir?"

"Why not; seems since Eleanor knows she'll inherit it she's even less attached to it than she was before. She's never here. I can't leave you anything, Joseph; I promised Eleanor, and as you know I'm trying to be a man of my word these days, so I'm giving you this now."

"Use of the house?" Joseph smirked.

"Sarcasm does not become you, Joseph."

"Sorry, sir," Joseph grinned, "it's not like you to be so, so…"

"So, humble, unselfish…you can say it. You can also say it's about time. No, Joseph, I would not insult you by giving you anything less than this." He held out his hand exposing a small silver key. "Anytime you get tired of me or feel like retiring, go to Biscoe Brothers International Bank and use it. I think you'll find it's your key to freedom. Now I'm going to find mine.

"And Joseph," he looked over his shoulder as he wobbled, toting two of his overstuffed valises. "I like you," he declared. "Perhaps you will want to come see this Mother Rose in a little while." Hefting, struggling and grunting, "You are not getting any younger yourself, you know."

Joseph smiled. Whatever had gotten Edward Steel had really gotten him. Perhaps there was something to this Lord and Savior thing.

Just Me

KIMBERLANE PULLED into the pier parking lot, her long wavy hair blowing with the breeze coming off the water. The time had come when she no longer cared if people thought she was white or knew she was black. She was just a happy, happy woman looking for her husband. "There he is," she pointed, her yellow-belled sleeve flapping with the wind.

"Where, where, Mommy?" Little Jimmy yelled. Jimmy was kinda yellow like his uncle Jasper, his brother Charlie had informed him.

"Right there." Charlie pointed to the bow of a boat.

"There," Kimberlane sighed. And there he stood wearing a captain's hat, a yellow-gold trimmed jacket—for effect—and matching nautical pants, standing erect and saluting no one in particular.

"An anniversary gift, my loves—we are going to sail the seven seas."

"Dad!" Charlie yelped.

"Or at least Lake Michigan," James responded. "All aboard," he said, stepping back on the pier and extending his hand for his small family to follow suit. "Ahem, attention, everyone," he continued, "Mommy's got an announcement."

"We already know Grandfather's coming," Charlie cut in hopping recklessly onto the boat.

"Yes, but so is someone else."

"Who? Not that mean Aunt Eleanor."

"NO!" James and Kimberlane howled together.

"How would you like a baby brother?"

"Do we have to?" questioned five-year-old Jimmy, Jr.

"Well, there's always a chance it's a girl," said his dad, pulling the little boy into his arms.

"Good, Mommy needs someone to help her around the house. Me and Charlie are tired. It can be her turn when she gets here."

"We won't put her to work right away; besides Daddy's thinking it's time for our little family to take a break...maybe do some traveling with Grandpa after the baby gets up some size."

"That's fine with me," Charlie responded. "Let's see what the other half lives like. " For some reason that struck his mother and father as funny; they laughed until they cried. Then the Johnsons sailed off into the sunset, together.

Love Dreams by Sherry Lucille,
second in a three-part trilogy.

Look for *Love Promises,*
coming soon.

Sherry is a passionate communicator and dynamic speaker. She is available for presentations and keynotes. You may purchase this book directly from the author, at bookstores near you, online and anytime!

Also visit www.sherrylucille.com or email sherrylucille@gmail.com for news of book signings and events

There are many dreams and many dreamers.
If you have the love of a good man, a man with humor, intelligence, industry, kindness, constancy and faith, one of real stuff and not of fairy fluff, then you have dreamed a good dream and been honored for it. Hold it tightly and never, never take it lightly.